Firm
Resolve

Licia Flynn

Published by Klar Marketing Communications

ISBN: 978-1-7322777-1-7

CONTENTS

CHARACTER INDEX

Aaron Walker – Ethnically ambiguous stranger at a club

Amy Liu – Cindy's best friend: Born in Beijing; marketing executive

Ben Chang – Curt's business partner; born in Fremont, California

Brian – Lana's Scandinavian friend

Bonnie – Office manager at a venture capital firm

Cal – High school peer of Natalia Canaan

Cindy Han – Cantonese marketing executive; grew up in the U.K

Colleen – Natalia's best friend

Conrad – Lead chemist at Curt's pharmaceutical company

Curt Steiger – Born in Germany; grew up in Chicago; PhD in chemistry; patent attorney

Daniel Petersen – Shanghai expat

Dara – Malaysian housekeeper

Eric – Works in the payroll department at the same law firm as Lana Hayaak

Gloria Rivers – Expat Women's Club member; former client of Daniel Petersen

Gretchen – Lana's friend in Shanghai; American medical doctor married to a finance manager

Gwen Karlson – Cindy and Amy's Swedish friend; tall, blonde, and age 19

Harold – Law student from the Midwest; works with Lana

Jakov Horvat – Security guard

Janet Perkins – Law firm office manager

Jason Canaan – Adopted from Korea; grew up in Maryland; Vietnam vet; Georgetown alum; architect

Kadir – Friendly guy at party

Kamlesh Khan – Curt's IT guy and friend of Lana; South Asian descent; from Nova Scotia

Karen – Lana's friend at the Expat Women's Club; Canadian corporate wife

Kay – Blonde student from Vancouver

Mr. Kelly – Canaan's young probate attorney

Kitty – Wife of Conrad (lead chemist at Curt's pharmaceutical company)

Lana Hayaak – Ethnically ambiguous law student

Lara Canaan – Adopted from Lithuania; grew up in Virginia; Georgetown alum; art dealer

Larry & Libby – Stray cat friends

Ludmilla – Beautiful Russian woman at a club Lana frequents

Matt – Marketing Director from Boston

Margaret – Natalia's classmate

Maria – Lana's law school friend

Milton Canaan – Natalia's third cousin

Natalia Canaan – Daughter of Jason and Lara Canaan

Mrs. Nowicki – Canaan's Polish neighbor

Paul – Club manager in Shanghai

Peter Lim – Vice President of a venture capital firm

Pierre – French guy at event

Priya Patel – Chemist at Curt's company

Rick – Associate at a venture capital firm

Sara – Lana's friend at the Expat Women's Club; teacher

Shelly – Lana's friend in Shanghai; British art teacher

Tomas Diaz – Brazilian journalist

Tracy – Lana's classmate in a constitutional law class

Troy Walker – Aaron's father; Vietnam vet

PROLOGUE
Shanghai — 2015

Déjà vu hit me as I entered the lobby, which made sense since I'd been to this venue in the past. However, today's nostalgia was unrelated to any party or event that I'd ever attended in Shanghai.

I walked past the reception desk and took the elevator to the 14th floor. While wandering through the hallways, my thoughts flickered back to 2009.

I suddenly heard, *"Nín yǒu shé me xūyào bāngmáng de ma?"*

Abruptly, I woke from my daydream and realized I was lost.

"Bù yòng xiè," I responded to an attendant who stood politely at the far end of a dark corridor.

Shanghai — 2017

Daniel Petersen's clothes were a mess. He looked worn and disheveled while sitting in the Shanghai police department. His dark beard was overgrown, and he smelled of liquor from a recent excursion.

Daniel stammered while reading a photocopied diary entry, which was covered in beer stains.

The detective listened patiently but finally interrupted. "Thank you for sharing, but what is your point?"

"I've already told you," Daniel snapped.

The detective finished his cigarette, leaned forward and asked, "Was there anything in *that* diary remotely relevant to this investigation?"

"Not exactly, but you can infer who had the incentive to murder her."

"Where were you when the *tai tai* disappeared?"

"What?"

The officer glared at him.

"Um … well I passed out after consuming —"

"Mr. Petersen, why were you drinking in the afternoon?"

"I wasn't. An admirer left a basket of caviar and chocolates in front of my door. I ate all of it and fell asleep."

"Admirer?" the detective asked with disbelief.

"Yeah," Daniel replied smiling. "I'm kind of popular with the ladies."

"I see."

"I'm debonair."

"Obviously," the detective lied. "So who was *this* admirer?"

"Some gal at the women's club, Mrs. Gloria Rivers."

"Did you verify that?"

"Nah, the doll has been after me for years. Who else could it have been?"

The detective exhaled and said cordially, "We appreciate your interest, but this case is closed."

"Why?"

"There's no trace of her. She's probably dead."

"But —"

"Mr. Petersen, I'm sorry to change the subject …"

The detective paused briefly to light a new cigarette. He offered one to Daniel who shook his head.

The detective continued, "We're well aware that you're working in China without a business visa."

"Huh," Daniel said with alarm.

"The government is becoming increasingly strict and is clamping down on these violations."

"Hey, are you threatening me?"

"Mr. Petersen, you need to leave. I advise that you either get a proper work permit or stop working in China."

Daniel got up and left without saying anything.

Later, a different detective entered and asked, "Was it that crazy *lao wai* again?"

"Yes, he's relentless."

"What does he do again?"

"Mr. Petersen lurks around Shanghai like a —"

"Bar fly?"

"Yes, a hairy insect."

PART 1
NATALIA CANAAN

CHAPTER 1
Kuala Lumpur — 1998

I didn't sleep the entire night. Instead, I sat on the steps of our colonial-style townhouse while mosquitoes devoured me. My skin was a mess of red wounds. Cicadas angrily cried as a stray cat scoured the streets howling for breakfast and a lizard ran past my feet.

I was soaking in sweat. Ordinarily I blamed Malaysia's heat, but this time, stress was the culprit.

Yesterday I slept late but jolted alert when I realized our home was unusually quiet. Impatiently, I jumped out of bed, raced down the hallway, and shouted for my parents because I knew something was wrong.

As I barged into their bedroom my fears actualized, because Mom and Dad were not there. Their bed was a mess. My heart raced, so I paused to catch my breath. I listened carefully but heard only birds chirping, water trickling in a nearby canal, and cars whizzing by.

I scurried down the stairs and crashed into the dining room, which was dead except for the hum of the Casablanca fan. The oriental carpet was out of place, and the entrance gate was wide open.

Alarmed, I quickly locked the front door. I flew to the back of the house and entered our kitchen, where suffocating humidity assaulted me. I glanced around the room, but fixated on an army of rapacious ants swarming across a big bowl of rotting mangoes, bananas, and guavas.

I returned to the living room, where the air-conditioning created condensation on the windows. I climbed up our teak-wood stairs, threw on a cotton dress, and dashed across the street to our neighbor's home. The sun burned furiously and palm trees swayed in the wind.

I jumped on to the Nowicki's marble front steps, which were guarded by two stone lions, and knocked impatiently.

A petite woman with a Slavic accent answered the door and asked gently, "Natalia, what's wrong?"

"Have you seen my parents?" I inquired a little too impatiently.

She shook her head no and said, "Aren't they at home with you?"

"Um, I thought Dad may have dropped by to talk to Mr. Nowicki about work," I replied, quickly realizing I should tailor the truth.

"There's no work these days," she reminded me. Dad and Mr. Nowicki were both architects. Their projects grinded to a halt when the crash hit in 1997.

"Yes, I don't know what I was thinking. I'm sorry to have troubled you."

"It's alright my dear."

I walked home with a chilling sense of dread.

CHAPTER 2

The Malaysian sun rose with fervor, but didn't alleviate my anxiety. However, I was relieved to see an olive-skinned woman with a cherubic face approach. Dara's black eyes widened with concern and her forehead furrowed when she saw me.

"Natalia, why are you sitting outside?"

"Dara, my parents are gone, and I can't find them anywhere."

Her eyes narrowed, but she was speechless.

"I called Dad's cell, but he didn't answer."

She nodded.

"Their car is gone. Should we call the police?" I asked.

My housekeeper shook her head firmly, but then said slowly, "Your parents went on a business trip."

"A trip?" I asked with skepticism.

"A secret trip," Dara whispered carefully, which made me think she was lying. However, I was eager to believe her.

"When will they return?"

"I'm not sure Natalia, but you need to leave Kuala Lumpur right now."

"How can I do that? I'm only fifteen and have three

years of high school left."

"Do you know how much money is in your parents' safe?"

"I have no idea," I exclaimed.

"We should find out," Dara ordered as she headed upstairs to my parents' room.

She opened the closet, pulled clothes to the side, and revealed a small safe.

"What's the code?"

"No clue," I responded.

"Figure it out and get the money. Then, go far away from here," Dara firmly instructed.

"Where do I go?" I asked softly.

"I don't know, but you don't have much time. You need to leave soon."

I reluctantly opened the safe after testing different numbers. I wasn't surprised to discover that the code was my birthday: 06 - 12 - 83. According to Mom and Dad, 1983 was a tumultuous year because of U.S. relations with the Soviet Union.

In the safe, I found some cash and jewelry.

CHAPTER 3

Dara and I took a taxi to the airport, but neither of us said much. I was grateful to her, but also fearful because I knew she was lying. My parents weren't on any trip.

As the taxi drove through the streets of Kuala Lumpur, I felt numb. Silently, I observed food stalls which sold tropical fruits such as durian, mangosteen, and rambutan. Other vendors hawked breakfast donuts and sweet, syrupy coffee. Schoolgirls in their crisp uniforms strolled by in clusters. We pulled up on to the modern highway, and I looked at the crowded skyscrapers against a hazy skyline. I wondered if this would be the last time I would ever see Malaysia.

When we arrived at the airport, I bought a one-way ticket to the United States. I checked two bulging suitcases filled with all of my belongings.

Dara walked me to security. "You'll go to your grandparents' home in Cincinnati?"

"Yes," I replied.

"At least, you'll be someplace safe," she said.

I hugged Dara tightly, wishing I didn't have to leave. I knew I might never see her again and worried about her future because she was now unemployed.

During my flight to San Francisco, I stressed over new problems. First, the Customs Declaration Form stated that one needed to declare sums greater than $10,000. I had $16,216.49 in my purse, which was all the money I possessed. I wondered if declaring this cash would mean losing it.

Second, my destination was not Ohio, because I didn't have any grandparents. In fact, I had never been to Cincinnati, even though my parents always told strangers that it was our hometown.

Both my parents were adopted as children and raised by elderly couples who had passed away. Dad spent his youth in Rockville, Maryland, while Mom grew up in Alexandria, Virginia. At least, that's what their official documents from the safe stated.

I didn't trust anything my parents told me, because they were never truthful with any of their friends. In public, they were outgoing and charismatic. At home, they were distant and emotionally unavailable.

As an only child, I had attended international schools in cities such as Berlin, Istanbul, and most recently Kuala Lumpur. Allegedly Dad was an architect and Mom was an art dealer, but neither was passionate about their work. Instead, they were preoccupied with issues that were far more complex than mainstream news stories such as the Iran-Contra Affair, Tiananmen, or the fall of the Berlin Wall. They constantly whispered about things I didn't understand.

***

When the plane landed at SFO, I felt apprehensive. People shoved me out of the way as I made my way to the crowded immigration line. A security guard spotted me, and his eyes narrowed while studying my face. *Did he know that I was carrying more than $10,000 of undeclared money?*

"Next," yelled an intimidating, heavy-set border agent who sat authoritatively behind a glass counter.

"Morning," I smiled brightly. I tried to emulate my mother's perky — albeit fake — style.

"Good morning," the officer grumbled while scrutinizing my face and flipping through my U.S. passport. "Are you traveling by yourself?"

"Yes, sir," I replied deferentially.

"You're a minor, where are you going?"

"Cincinnati."

"Shouldn't you be in school?"

"I'll start next week."

"Where are your parents?"

"Dad met this young, pretty woman in Malaysia. They became best friends, and Mom was quite —"

Abruptly the immigration officer cut me off. "I don't need the details. Are you carrying anything given to you by someone else?"

"No."

"Are you carrying more than $10,000?"

"Nope," I lied.

"Okay, welcome home, Natalia." He handed the customs form back to me.

"Thank you."

I collected my bags and sauntered up to a customs officer, who collected my form with disinterest.

However, as I approached the exit, I sensed danger. I stopped, turned, and saw a tall security guard with red hair and freckles approaching. He ran up and peered into my eyes.

My body tensed, and my hands trembled.

"Miss, you dropped your scarf," the guard said kindly.

"Oh, thank you," I exclaimed, as my cheeks turned red.

"Be careful, a pretty young girl like you could get hurt."

I gasped, *Was this a threat or a warning?*

"Have a nice day," he said smiling.

Impatiently, I marched through the security doors where people welcomed friends and family. *At least I don't have to deal with that drama*, I thought sardonically.

I dragged my luggage upstairs, bolted up to a ticketing agent and asked, "Can I change my flight?"

"That'll cost you extra," a terse agent replied.

"Okay," I agreed.

"Where do you want to go?"

"Portland ..." I responded. "Portland, Oregon."

CHAPTER 4
Portland, Oregon

A cab drove me to a house at the end of a cul-de-sac on a street lined with maple trees. My father sort of inherited it a year ago. Subsequently my parents repeatedly said, "Natalia, if we're ever separated, go to the residence in Oregon and we'll find you."

We spent last July at this creepy place after completing piles of paperwork. I didn't understand the legalities, but Dad received something called a "life estate."

FLASHBACK 1997

In the conference room of our lawyer's office, I sat quietly and listened.

Dad said, "Let me get this straight; I have a life-estate in the property I recently inherited?"

His young, somewhat nervous attorney replied, "That's correct, Mr. Canaan. Upon your death, this house will pass to your third-cousin, Milton Canaan."

"That's great, so I have nothing to leave my daughter?" Dad asked sharply.

"Well, you can leave her your own personal property, but not the

Portland home," Mr. Kelly explained.

My mother interjected, "Jason, at least you inherited something. All I got was debt when Mom and Dad died."

Dad wasn't pacified and snapped, "Nah, this is bullshit. Milton meant nothing to my parents. I'm getting stiffed because I'm not a blood relation."

"Jason, it's a place we can live rent-free," Mom suggested.

Ignoring her, Dad said, "Mr. Kelly, I want to set up a life insurance policy. In case I die, I want to make sure my wife and daughter are taken care of."

"Certainly Mr. Canaan, I'm happy to take care of that."

Sitting in the taxi, I pondered my predicament. To collect on the life insurance, I had to prove that Dad was dead. However, then I couldn't stay in this life-estate. Plus, I had no relatives, except for Milton who was hardly family. Ending up in foster care was my worst nightmare, so pretending Mom and Dad were around, but rarely here seemed like my only option. That way, I could live in this house — at least for a while.

***

The taxi sped off while I stood in the driveway with my luggage. In the dark, the old Victorian home looked black and tattered like something out of a horror film.

I rustled through my suitcase looking for the bag of keys I had found in the safe. Impatiently, I experimented with different ones. My thoughts raced as I tried key after key. A week ago, my biggest concern was what I would wear when school started. Now I had far greater issues.

Finally, a key unlocked the door, and I entered darkness. None of the lights worked, so I stumbled into the living room and collapsed on a dusty velvet sofa in my dirty clothes.

CHAPTER 5

I woke to the sound of rain splattering against the windows. Dehydrated, I wandered into the kitchen where brown sludge gushed from the faucet. I rummaged through cabinets and found bottles of sparkling water. I aggressively twisted off a cap and guzzled. There were cans of soup, beans, and baby corn on shelves in the pantry. But I wasn't hungry.

I hadn't showered since leaving Malaysia. I felt the same way I used to after a night out with friends in KL. Since ninth grade, my classmates had frequently thrown parties that typically began in hotel ballrooms and ended at clubs in the heart of the city. I always smelled of cigarette smoke and whiskey after those escapades.

I threw on my jacket and ventured into the damp, empty street. The crisp air of Oregon was a stark contrast to the warmth I had known for years. I took a bus to the local YMCA and registered as a new member so that I could finally shower.

While washing my hair, I observed other members whose gray hair and wrinkles suggested wisdom and maturity. They talked about the environment, the war in

Yugoslavia, and some guy named Ralph Nader. In contrast, Mom's expat friends sported fashionable designs and expensively dyed hair. They chatted about shopping, plastic surgery, and extra-marital affairs.

Standing in the old locker room, I quickly dressed. As I climbed into my jeans, I thought about money. I wanted to talk to Dad's lawyer but didn't think I could afford his fees. Besides, what would I say? More importantly, could I even trust him?

After leaving the Y, I went on a long walk to the public library, which gave me time to think. In order to get running electricity and water, I'd call the utilities company and pretend to be Mom. Our old account from last year would be on record.

When I arrived at the library, I managed to find a vacant computer. Sandwiched between homeless men who smelled of liquor, I thought about emailing Dara. I carefully crafted an email, but got scared and wondered if this was a good idea. Who might be able to read my emails? Would they then figure out my whereabouts? I trashed the message and performed some perfunctory Internet searches. According to my findings, after a seven-year absence, I could collect Dad's life insurance benefits.

Later, I wandered into a convenience store and bought a phone card. I called Dara twice, from a phone booth, but her line was disconnected.

As I headed home, I considered things. I wouldn't turn sixteen until next year, so finding a job besides babysitting would be difficult. I thought about renting out rooms in the house, since there were four additional ones, but that would be risky. If a tenant caused trouble, or if my cousin found out, I could end up in foster care. So for now, I had to support myself through babysitting.

When I finally got home, with a bag of fruit, nuts, and soymilk, the sun was setting, so I lit a few candles.

CHAPTER 6

I sat in the registrar's office of the local high school. A woman with curly gray hair, blue eyes, and thick glasses listened to me as I nervously babbled.

"Where did you say you're from?" she asked while studying my face thoughtfully.

I was used to this reaction from strangers. I figured instinctively that she was confused about my ethnicity. My features were as ambiguous as my mannerisms and accent.

My voice faltered as I said, "San Francisco."

I wanted to keep things simple because my background confused most people. Thing is, except for passing through the airport, I had only spent a weekend in the Bay Area when I was ten.

"Ah, okay, that makes sense," the woman murmured under her breath.

I continued talking, "Mom moved up here to focus on her artwork because Dad met this younger woman —"

The registrar cut me off gently. "It's okay Natalia, no need to explain. Classes began last week, but we have space for you in Mr. McCann's homeroom."

CHAPTER 7

A few weeks after starting school, I was at home sitting in my dusty attic filled with cobwebs and dark shadows. Every crack in the ceiling hinted at a story.

I quickly flipped through a photo album of my parents, which was one of the few sentimental items of theirs that I possessed. I studied a photo of them taken in 1979. Born in Lithuania, Mom was blonde with green eyes. Born in Korea, Dad had sharp cheekbones, a square jaw, and a golden tan.

I glanced at the mantle and studied my father's medals from his service in Vietnam. Dad was a decorated soldier who had survived prisoner-of-war camps. But instead of a military career, he used the GI bill to get a degree in architecture.

I was born in Kuwait but had lived in Berlin, Istanbul, and most recently Kuala Lumpur.

My parents were not religious having rejected their upbringing. Nevertheless, certain beliefs and attitudes were inescapable. Mom was kind, but viewed the world in binary terms. Dad was cold-tempered, but harsh when challenged.

Their childhood stories filled me with anxiety, because I

was fiercely independent and preferred the anonymity that I didn't think was possible in a big family.

I woke early each day to squeeze in a few miles of running. However, in the last few weeks, I began to feel as if someone was watching me. I wasn't sure, but I swore that I had seen a dark car appear daily at different parts of my route.

In the evening, I often thought I heard rustling in the bushes outside of my window. It felt like someone was watching me, but I never saw anyone. I hoped it was a deer, raccoon, or my overactive imagination.

CHAPTER 8
1999

I furiously scribbled notes during history, my favorite class of the day. I glanced up as the clock struck 3 p.m. The bell rang, and I gathered my books. As I walked out of the crowded classroom to get to my locker, a lanky guy with auburn hair approached.

"Hey Natalia, what's up?"

"Not much, how are you Cal?"

"I was wondering if you wanted to go to Springfest with me."

"Um, thanks, but I can't."

"Why?"

"I've gotta help my parents with their business."

"Yeah, right."

"Excuse me?"

"I don't think you have any parents," Cal declared with a sneer.

"I have to go," I said tersely.

I shut my locker and walked outside where it was chilly. I could smell fresh grass and Douglas fir trees.

"Natalia, wait up!"

I turned and saw my best friend. Colleen was a tall, slender blonde with green eyes and freckles.

"Natalia, what's wrong with you?"

"What do you mean?"

"Why don't you want to go to the festival with Cal?"

"I constantly see him lurking around like a criminal."

"C'mon Natalia, he's not so bad."

"Then you should go out with him," I suggested.

"I know you like Peter, but he has a girlfriend."

"I don't know what you're talking."

"Peter is a flirt, so don't get the wrong idea."

I ignored Colleen and said, "I thought you were going to the Springfest with me."

"Sure, but you just told Cal that you have to work for your parents."

"Oops, I don't know what I was thinking."

"It's okay. Maybe it's better if neither of us goes. We can rent a movie or something."

I didn't realize that as we were talking our friend Margaret had snuck up behind us. She had dark-brown hair, big brown eyes, and a stocky frame.

"You're both scared," Margaret taunted.

"What are you talking about?" I asked.

"If you weren't afraid, then you'd go to the festival," she replied.

"This from someone who sleeps with her light on." I joked.

"How do you know that?" Margaret demanded.

"At 5 a.m., the light in your room is still on."

"Natalia, you shouldn't be jogging when it's dark. That's dangerous," Colleen advised.

"Yeah, I keep seeing this car popping up during my jogs," I admitted.

Colleen exclaimed, "That's creepy. Go to the Y or something."

"The old hippies get too chatty," I complained.

"Yeah, they're high on life," Margaret explained.

"They're high on something," I remarked absent-mindedly.

"Yeah, you oughta try it … 'cuz you need to chill out," Margaret teased.

"I've got a lot on my mind," I confessed.

"Don't we all?" Colleen asked.

"Uh, huh," I agreed, "I'll see you two later. I've got to get to my babysitting job."

"Alright Natalia, see ya," they both chimed.

As I left, I looked up and observed that the sky was overcast. If I didn't hurry, I'd get caught in the rain. I thought about what Cal said. How did he know about my parents' absence? Had he been stalking me?

Even if I wanted to go to Springfest, I really couldn't because I didn't have enough money. Babysitting barely covered my bills.

I rushed down the sidewalk as a squirrel dragged a baguette through the grass. I was about to cross a driveway when a car startled me by pulling up out of nowhere. A man rolled down his window, leaned forward, and yelled, "Hey, how are you?"

I gasped with fear and hurried to get home, but the car followed. I ran, but when I reached my house at the end of the cul-de-sac, the same vehicle pulled into my driveway. The man quickly jumped out and barked, "Natalia? Natalia Canaan?"

I stood speechlessly. I wasn't sure if I should race into my house or run towards the opposite street. Unfortunately, this stranger was blocking my path.

The man approached and said, "Natalia, my name is Milton. I'm your cousin."

This was not my day, I thought. I regretted not darting across the street when I had the chance. It was too late now because I was trapped.

"Milton, so lovely to meet you," I chirped with fake

enthusiasm. I extended my hand professionally the way my parents did with business associates.

He ignored my gesture and declared, "I've been messaging Jason for almost a year. Is your father home?"

I shook my head. "Dad isn't here right now, but I promise to tell him you stopped by."

Milton looked annoyed and asked, "Can I wait inside? Technically, it is *my* house."

Nervously, I stammered, "Dad would kill me if I let an unfamiliar man inside."

"I'm not a stranger; I'm your cousin," he retorted.

Ha, like a fourth cousin and not by blood, I silently mused. Aloud I said, "You know Dad … he'd kill me."

It was evident that Milton couldn't care less what punishment I might receive. However, he wasn't eager for further confrontation.

There was an awkward silence as we stared at one another. Finally, he handed me his business card and said, "Have your dad contact me."

"Sure," I lied. "Sorry, but I have to get to my babysitting job." I then ran across the street.

From a distance, I could see my cousin lingering. He meticulously inspected the place as if it was his. He peered into various rain-stained windows and crept to the back of the garden, which was filled with weeds and had a broken swing.

It was unlikely I would ever inherit the house from Milton, because he had been married twice and had four kids. Plus, according to Dad, he was a spendthrift with gambling debts.

I scurried over to the library where I created a fake email account for Dad and wrote:

Dear Milton,
Sorry for being out of touch. I lost my job and was traveling a lot for interviews.

I'm now very sick with mounting medical bills. Can I borrow $20,000? As you know, I have to care for my family. Plus, the house needs repairs.
Thank you,
Jason

As I hoped, Milton didn't respond. Six months later, to ensure that he remained at bay, I sent another email:

Hey Milton,
I'll be in your area, soon. Let's meet for coffee. I have this great idea for a business. Hope you will partner or invest.
Cheers,
Jason

Again, I didn't hear back. I knew my relative would eventually return, but at least I could try to stall him until I finished high school.

PART 2
2009

CHAPTER 1
Curt Steiger

The rains poured intermittently while I sat at my office desk in Hong Kong reading documents. I looked up as a senior partner barged in and said, "Curt, did you see those patent applications I left on your desk last night?"

"Yes, I reviewed them and think —"

"Hold on a second, I need to speak with another associate," he mumbled and ran off.

While waiting for my boss to return, I checked Facebook quickly and noticed a post by my former classmate, Lana Hayaak. She was a year behind me and had a summer job in Shanghai. I was envious because I wanted a position on the Mainland.

I was taken aback the first time I saw Lana because she didn't look like a law student. I don't remember what she wore, but it was conservative yet stylish. She reminded me of an actress from a black-and-white film Mom watched when I was growing up in the Midwest.

Lana had black hair, a fair-skinned oval face, and almond-shaped eyes. Her features were delicately chiseled and defined by details such as a widow's peak, accentuated lips with a cupid's bow, high cheekbones, and a pointed nose.

In the heart of Silicon Valley, characterized by cutting-edge technology, innovation, and masculinity, Lana was like a wildflower in the middle of the law school's neatly manicured lawn. In other words, she didn't entirely belong.

FLASHBACK 2008

Last August, I was on my way to a corporate law class when I saw Lana running up the path. She looked troubled as she tried to balance casebooks while clutching her laptop bag. Accidentally, her skirt had gotten hiked up, and she looked embarrassed while struggling to adjust it.

When I got to class I chose a seat directly behind Lana who was busy organizing her notes. She opened her laptop, and an electronic cat popped up and cried loudly. I expected our Professor to be irritated, but he turned to her, laughed, and asked, "Is that your cat?" She nodded shyly.

The class became suddenly quiet as our professor began to lecture:

"Dodge claimed that Ford was abusing power because he had no justifiable business reason for refusing to distribute dividends. Can someone please tell me why Ford chose to do this?"

Eager hands, including my own, shot up. Our professor glanced around the room, but his eyes fell upon the woman in front of me. "Lana?" he asked with a grin.

"Ford wanted to benefit society," she answered.

"Um, no," Professor Beale said. He looked disappointed. "Someone else?"

Classmates around me raised their hands aggressively like hungry hawks lunging in for the kill.

I raised mine and said, "Henry Ford wanted to discontinue dividends for shareholders in order to increase investments in other plants. That way Ford Motor Company could dramatically increase production thereby decreasing costs and the prices of cars."

Professor Beale nodded and said, "Excellent, Curt."

After class was over, swarms of students flocked to the instructor's side like an order of angry flies.

As I walked out of class I tried to catch Lana's eye, but she didn't see me. I figured she was embarrassed by her weak answer. She ventured over to the library, so I followed her up a flight of Spanish-tile steps. Lana strolled into the office of an international law professor who was visiting from a leading Midwestern university.

I could hear everything because the door was wide open:

"Professor Fitzgerald, I have serious issues with the assigned reading."

"What's the problem, Lana?"

"With all due respect, it's apologist propaganda."

"If you have a problem with my syllabus then you can take it up with the Board of Trustees."

"I don't want to do that," she exclaimed.

"Lana, I was teasing you. I have survived numerous Deans at my own law school. This one is uniquely tolerant."

"We're lucky to have you."

"Thank you, I'm happy to be here."

"Professor Fitzgerald, what was it like representing the North African leader—"

I was now bored by this conversation and walked away as I heard Lana mention the name of a notorious dictator.

A few hours later, I saw her studying at a table outside the library. She stopped reading to watch a pair of squirrels chase one another up a palm tree. I took the opportunity to approach and said,

"Hey Lana, what do you think of our corporate law class?"

"It's alright," she said with hesitation. "I'm sorry, but I forgot your name."

"Curt Steiger."

"That's German, isn't it?"

"Yes, I was born in Stuttgart, but moved to Chicago when I was eight." I was surprised by her interest, because no one ever cared.

"You don't have a German accent," Lana observed with the playful curiosity of a kitten.

"Ah, well, as children we lose our accent if we learn English before age nine."

Lana nodded, then with a coy expression said, "Doesn't Steiger mean 'womanizer' in German?"

"It doesn't," I protested with mild irritation, "It means 'to climb.'"

"I see." Lana grinned and asked, "But what do you seek to climb?"

I ignored her silliness. "I'm kind of struggling with corporate law. Do you think you could tutor me?" This was a lie because I was at the top of my class. If anyone needed help, it was Lana.

She looked flattered, smiled brightly, and exclaimed, "Sure, Curt, I would love to help you."

Not with your C average, I thought snidely. This was guaranteed to be fun.

I heard bold footsteps approaching. The senior partner was back and said, "Steiger, this will have to wait until Monday. Please go home."

I packed my briefcase and left the office while thinking about my career. Six months ago, I was a pharmaceutical scientist and part-time law student. Now, I was an IP attorney at a leading firm. I liked my practice but envisioned a more powerful future.

I crossed the congested intersection and headed up the hill towards *Lan Kwai Fong*, a trendy European district. I was meeting Cindy, an old friend, for dinner. Despite being an hour late, I didn't worry much because she was always a great sport.

CHAPTER 2
June 2009

An elegant woman with black hair, golden skin, and cat-like eyes stealthily made her way through the dark alleyways of Shanghai's *Bund* district. Cindy was in her early thirties but looked younger.

Sleek like a panther, the lithe, fashionable woman walked briskly to a nightclub by the riverside. After climbing the marble stairs of a colonial-style building and entering a room filled with an after-work crowd, she headed toward the terrace.

Cindy approached a lanky blonde man and asked, "Hi, are you, the manager?"

He turned around and with a leisurely drawl said, "Yep, the name's Paul and who might you be?"

"Cindy," she replied with a crisp British accent.

"Beautiful name. I once had a girlfriend named Cindy."

"Um, thank you."

"Let me get you a drink," Paul insisted while leading her towards the outdoor bar where a pack of men ogled a small party of women on the dance floor.

"Isn't it Ladies' Night? I mostly see guys."

"Quite an understatement," Paul responded as he handed Cindy a gaudy looking cocktail.

"Thank you," she said while accepting her drink.

"Why are you here alone?"

"I'm not," Cindy responded. She looked over at her colleagues who were sitting at a low glass table covered with drinks.

Paul looked very disappointed. "So why aren't you with them?"

"Jakov told me that you know everyone in town."

"You've been chatting up the Slavs, eh?"

"Why not?" Cindy replied with a sly grin.

"Yeah, I know all the night crawlers," Paul admitted.

"Do you know a woman named Lana?"

"Yep, she comes here a lot."

"So she's quite the party animal?"

"Not exactly. Actually, she's kind of an odd bird."

"What do you mean?" Cindy inquired while delicately sipping her drink.

Paul paused for a minute and gulped his chardonnay before declaring, "She's a lesbian."

Cindy was surprised by his statement. She regretted not sending Amy to do her dirty work. However, her best friend had flatly refused insisting that this investigation was a "pointless endeavor."

After a deep breath, Cindy asked, "Why do you think she's gay?"

"Experience. I'm an expert on women," Paul bragged.

The club's volume had dramatically increased. Thus, she practically had to shout, "Are you friends with her?"

"Nah, she's a total bitch."

"Really?"

"I walked up to Lana one night and asked her to join me for a drink, but she brushed me away like I worked here and stormed off."

"But you do work here," Cindy reminded the manager.

Paul's initially upbeat mood was now replaced with irritability. Glancing towards the door, he snapped, "I've gotta go. My girlfriend just arrived."

Cindy observed a young Eastern European brunette enter and remarked, "She's stunning."

"Yeah, but she's nuts."

"She looks sane to me," Cindy countered.

"If she sees us talking, you'll see crazy," Paul promised.

"Thanks for the drink," Cindy said and joined her group of friends.

CHAPTER 3
May 2009
Lana Hayaak

"Lana, get to the Chinese Embassy before 9 a.m.," my classmate, Tracy, suggested.

I climbed Cathedral Hill early, but a long line had already formed by the time I arrived. I get mocked whenever I tell people that San Francisco is cold, but on this particular day in May it was truly freezing.

Chinese instrumental music played in the background. I felt guilty that I wasn't studying. However, it wasn't easy to read a textbook while standing, so I pulled out a paperback novel.

I was trying to focus when a young guy on a skateboard rolled up and analyzed me.

"What are you reading?" he asked.

"*The Game*," I responded. "It's a guide for pursuing women."

"Uh, huh," the kid murmured while scanning the back flap of my book.

"It's very popular in Europe," I continued.

"Why would European men need that? Aren't they the

masters of seduction?"

I shrugged my shoulders and replied, "Good point."

"So why are you reading it?"

"I want a different perspective," I joked.

He listened intently and asked, "Why are you going to China?"

"I have a summer job in Shanghai. And you?"

"I'm heading there to buy a private jet."

Looking at his rusty skateboard, I smiled and said, "Nice."

He grinned and confessed, "I never go anywhere. I just process visas for companies."

I nodded and continued reading.

"What's your name?" he asked.

"Gertrude."

"Do you have a Facebook account?"

I shook my head and lied, "I disabled it."

He looked offended.

"I'm too old for you," I explained.

The visa runner pushed his way through the line to get away from me.

I never enjoy these types of encounters; however, I was distracted by other concerns. The Chinese Embassy's visa application form required a listing of all "former names." All I could think was, *Did anyone need to know that my birth name was Natalia Canaan?*

***

I was late when I got back to campus because processing my visa took most of the day.

As I entered the arena-style classroom, my professor said, "Lana, tell us about *Nguyen v. Texas.*"

"Sure," I responded while struggling to open my laptop. But it was frozen, like a stalled car in the middle of an intersection. I frantically grabbed my casebook, but couldn't find the right page.

"Lana, we're waiting."

I heard giggles from across the room. My cheeks swelled while I felt glances in my direction.

Sitting in front of me, my girlfriend Tracy swung around and whispered, "Lana, get on IM. I'll message you the answers."

"Lana?"

Finally, I responded, "*Nguyen v. Texas* is about a man convicted of sexual assault. Nguyen risked deportation to Vietnam, because he was not a U.S. citizen. He was the illegitimate son of a U.S. soldier and a Vietnamese citizen. Nguyen's mother abandoned him and he moved to Texas at age six where he grew up with his biological father."

My professor nodded. "What was the issue?"

"Whether citizenship based on the child's mother or father's nationality violates the *Equal Protection Clause*?"

"And does it?"

I replied, "It doesn't violate the *Equal Protection Clause* because when a child is born overseas and out of wedlock, strict proof of paternity rather than maternity is constitutionally required to prove the child's citizenship if the child is born to only one citizen parent."

My professor nodded and turned to question someone else.

I thought about *Nguyen v. Texas*. As far as I was concerned, this was a sex-discrimination case because fathers were treated differently than mothers. Yet I had never heard any outrage about it.

The court reasoned that it's easier to prove a biological relationship between a mother and her child; as opposed to the father. However, I bet this wouldn't happen in patriarchal countries.

I disagreed with the court because there was something inherently unfair about deporting someone to a foreign country after his biological father had raised him in the United States for most of his life.

After class, Tracy said, "Lana, I felt so sorry for you."

"Thanks for trying to help me."

"Hey, what've you got there?" she asked, eyeing my novel.

"Just fun reading," I said quickly, stuffing my novel into my bag.

"You love fiction, don't you?"

"There's more truth in fiction than nonfiction."

"That makes no sense," Tracy joked while walking away.

As I headed home in the dark, I passed the historic Spanish Mission church and thought about the case discussed in class. Nguyen was mixed race which was ubiquitous in California. However, growing up, I didn't meet very many Eurasians — persons of mixed European and Asian ancestry — except while living in Berlin. Remembering Europe always triggered memories of Mom and Dad.

I had expected to read about my parents in the KL newspaper, which I accessed online at the public library. For years, I followed current events in Malaysia. I thought I would read about police hunts, volunteer efforts, and theories concerning their disappearance. But there was nothing.

I fantasized that either parent might show up on my doorstep, but it never happened. I had almost given up, except for the faint hope that Mom and Dad could be in China. While neither had ever been there, it had long been a source of intrigue for both. Dad spoke Mandarin and Mom was an expert on the Far East.

During winter break I sent out numerous applications to law firms in China. I preferred a position in Beijing, but the only response I received was from a firm in Shanghai.

CHAPTER 4

I hit my alarm and fell back in bed. Exams had finished a few days ago, so having nothing to do, I hugged my pillow and drifted back to sleep. But I woke suddenly and panicked when I remembered that I had a flight to catch.

As the temperatures in Silicon Valley soared, I ran out of my apartment like a lunatic and took off for SFO.

The flight to China was over ten hours long. During a brief layover in Seoul, I took a seat in an empty area at my gate. While reading my book, *A Foreigner's Guide to Shanghai*, a man slipped into the chair opposite from me.

"You look like a tourist," he scoffed.

"I guess," I replied, as I looked up to see a young man with curly dark hair and sapphire colored eyes. I couldn't help noticing that he had the type of smooth skin that most women desire. In fact, his complexion rivaled that of the Korean model in the poster by the Duty-Free section of Incheon International Airport.

He chuckled. "Let me guess, this is your first time to China?"

"How did you know?"

"No one who's ever been to China would be so blatant

about being … fresh off the boat."

"Right," I murmured as I ran off to the restroom.

While walking through the immaculately clean airport, I thought about Dad because he was born in Korea over sixty years ago. He spent at least three years at an orphanage before his adoption.

Twenty minutes later, after boarding the plane, I heard a familiar voice quip, "Well, well … so we meet again."

"It's a small plane," I noted while sitting down in an aisle seat next to the stranger I met at the gate.

"Why Shanghai?"

"I'm visiting my husband."

"Your husband?" he asked with disbelief.

"Yes," I insisted.

"Wearing that much perfume?"

I didn't know what to say, so I reached into my bag to find my headphones.

"My name is Daniel, what's yours?"

I sighed, took a deep breath and said, "Ralph."

"Ralph? Your name is not really Ralph."

"Yes, my name is really Ralph," I lied. "My father always wanted a son, but got me instead."

"Okay, Really Ralph, nice to meet you. But I think I'll call you Batman."

I put on my headphones and increased the volume. When the plane landed, I jumped up to get my carry-on from the overhead bin.

I was going to ignore Daniel, but on reconsideration asked, "Do you want me to retrieve your luggage from the overhead bin?"

He grinned and said, "Are you trying to emasculate me?"

I smiled, turned to follow exiting passengers, and briskly walked off the plane.

Daniel chased after me and said, "Batman, since we're both strangers in this foreign country, let's exchange numbers."

"I'd love to, but I don't have a phone."

"C'mon, one coffee, what's the worst that could happen?"

"Um," I stammered.

"At the very least, we'd have a horror story to tell our friends."

"Your friends must hear a lot of stories," I joked.

Daniel pulled out his business card, handed it to me, and said, "Call me, Batman."

***

I exited immigration, entered the airport's arrival section, and saw an older man in a gray uniform holding a sign with my name on it. I walked up, introduced myself, and he enthusiastically welcomed me. I followed him to a company van where he loaded my luggage.

As the van flew down the highways of Shanghai, I gazed at the city. It was a paradoxical mixture of ancient and modern, as well as Western and Eastern.

An hour later, we pulled up to a tall tower. The driver opened the door and I hopped out. We passed through glass doors and walked across marble floors. The concierge briefly acknowledged us as my escort barked something I didn't comprehend.

Minutes later, I was greeted by Janet Perkins, the office manager of the law firm where I would work.

"Lana, we meet at last," she said.

"Ms. Perkins, it's great to meet you."

"Please, call me Janet and now follow me with your things." She took me to an apartment on the 10th floor.

"This is such an exquisite place," I remarked appreciatively.

"Before you get too comfortable, there's some bad news," Janet warned.

"Bad news?"

"The authorities recently blocked Facebook, but don't worry. We're working it out. You'll soon have access."

I was less surprised about the government blocking Facebook than I was about the fact that my boss encouraged using it.

CHAPTER 5

Giddy from jet lag, I woke early the next morning and ventured into the shopping complex near Janet's apartment. Local workers were already bustling: city cleaners swept the streets, shopkeepers prepped their stores, and maids polished windows.

Unfortunately, by the time I arrived at the office, my buzz had worn off and sleepiness overtook me. As I sat in Janet's HR office in the back corner of the firm in the *Changing* district, I felt like I had been hit over the head with a pile of legal hornbooks. She talked, but I couldn't hear her because my thoughts were drowning in an ocean of chaos.

"Lana, here's a list of events," Janet instructed.

"Events?" I asked.

Janet looked impatient. "Yes, these are professional networking events you need to attend after work."

"Um, okay," I said. I felt overwhelmed. If Janet had asked me to go to an event, earlier this morning, say at 3 a.m. when I first woke, I would have been overjoyed. But now at 9:45 a.m., I just wanted to crash. There had been way too much sugar in the coffee I purchased from a local vendor. I felt nauseous.

"Alright, Lana, let me introduce you to everyone in your department." Janet stood up and officially marched me through the office. As we took the stairs to a different floor, she continued, "You'll be working in the commercial litigation department with local attorneys."

"Cool, I love litigation," I expressed with girlish enthusiasm.

Janet turned and gave me a strange look. I responded with a nervous smile.

CHAPTER 6

After a week of being in Shanghai, I had almost recovered from jet-lag because I no longer fell asleep at 9 p.m. and woke at 3 a.m.

It was noon, and I decided not to join my co-workers for lunch at *Hooters*, a popular venue across the street because the food was terrible and overpriced. Frankly, I couldn't understand its attraction.

I was standing by my desk reading a local take-out menu when a friendly guy from payroll stopped by my cubicle. I looked up and asked, "Eric, you're not going to *Hooters*?"

"God no," he replied with disgust. "Lana, you'll find that Shanghai can be a very lonely place."

I was struck by his candor and remarked, "But we're surrounded by millions of people."

"Yeah, but they're very inaccessible."

I nodded.

Eric continued, "You might want to make friends outside of work."

"I don't really know anyone except some guy I met on the plane."

Eric smiled and said, "Give him a call, but just

remember that expats in China are not always who they pretend to be."

"Sure, so it's safer to be friends with people you meet through school or work, right?"

Eric shook his head firmly and advised, "Don't get too close to anyone at work."

I nodded.

"I've got to get back to crunching numbers, but I'll see you later, Lana."

"Okay, bye Eric."

It would be at least fifteen minutes before my lunch of rice and vegetables was delivered, so I rifled through my purse and found Daniel's business card. I hastily sent off an email:

Hi, it's the woman from the plane.

Instantly, Daniel responded:

Batman, I knew I'd hear from you. Give me your cell number.

I wrote back:

Let's keep this to email.

Daniel:

No way, Batman, I'll call you, and we'll talk like two adults. Now, let's have the digits.

I replied:

Okay, but please don't call me until after 7 p.m.

As I was walking down the street, on my way to the subway, Daniel called. "So Batman, I think we've got a problem."

"What problem?"

"I looked you up online. You've gotta be at least twenty-five. That's a real problem for me because I only date younger women."

Without hesitation, I hit *end call*, and Daniel's words faded away.

CHAPTER 7

Cindy was at home in her chic studio apartment located in the heart of the *Jing'an* District. It was a warm Saturday afternoon, and she was trying to fry egg noodles with one hand while holding her cell phone with the other.

"I'm not your spy," she snapped.

Cindy listened to the person on the phone for a few minutes and then said, "I don't have time."

She turned off the stove and paced the room, trying to focus on her conversation.

Finally, Cindy said, "Not so far, but I'll let you know what happens."

She then hung up the phone without saying goodbye.

Filled with irritation, Cindy threw her burnt food into the trash and opened the window to air out the fumes. Having lost her appetite, she threw on her Burberry raincoat and headed out of her apartment.

As Cindy waited for the elevator, in the open air hallway, she used her cell phone to make a call. "Alright, how many shares do I need to buy?"

The elevator opened and Cindy entered while listening to the person whom she had called. Finally, she responded,

"No, I don't care about that. Just make sure I'm a controlling shareholder."

CHAPTER 8

The following week, I left an event early due to a headache. I suspect that I was sick from inhaling so much cigarette smoke.

Janet was on holiday in Bali, so I hoped that she wouldn't know about my early departure.

I stumbled around the pantry searching for decongestants before returning to my laptop, where I discovered an email from a classmate:

Lana,
I'm in Hong Kong but will be in Shanghai soon. Let's meet up.
Best, Curt.

I didn't know Curt very well, but he was a fairly tall guy in his thirties. Everyone seemed to like him. Professors favored him, women laughed at his jokes, and men agreed with his points.

I, on the other hand, was not so easily impressed. Steiger annoyed me with his wavy brown hair, crystal blue eyes, and pearly white smile. He reminded me of a guy in a toothpaste commercial or a Congressional rep on C-SPAN.

I imagined that Curt grew up in a pretty house with a white picket fence and loved playing any sport that featured a ball and was always picked first for any team.

In contrast, I never cared for sports involving something that could hit me in the face. I preferred pursuits like running, ice skating, and swimming. I avoided big-toothy grins like Curt's because I didn't like showing my teeth. And I had never lived in a house with a white picket fence unless you counted my cousin's place in Portland. I didn't because the wooden gate was rotting from termite infestation, constant rain, and lack of upkeep.

Curt sat behind me in a corporate law course filled with PhDs. I once overheard his friend joke, "Why pay for a date? Wouldn't it be more expeditious to give a woman fifty bucks for sex? After all, isn't a date payment for sex?"

Curt was stoic and didn't engage in adolescent discussions. However, I felt he was guilty by association. Curt volunteered whenever cases pertained to pharmaceutical and biotech issues. On a macro-level, I disagreed with him, but refrained from any form of debate because he fixated on minutiae that I didn't fully understand. Rather than risk public ridicule, I kept my opinions to myself.

I ignored Steiger's message and focused on picking out an outfit to wear to work the next day. I gravitated towards classic styles and typically wore dark pencil skirts, white blouses, and flats.

As I got ready for bed, I thought about Malaysia because living in Shanghai triggered repressed memories. KL rapidly developed in the nineties, as China had for the past decade. However, the 1997 Asian financial crisis drastically changed our lifestyle and security. My parents began fighting because Dad had invested his savings in a fraudulent hedge fund.

Lying in bed, I struggled to fall asleep. I was wound up, and could hear my neighbors quarreling in Mandarin because the apartment walls were deceptively thin. Their squabbles sounded familiar, and as I drifted off, I heard my mother screaming, *"Jason, how could you? How could you trust our life savings with such an obvious crook?"*

CHAPTER 9

On Thursday night, I joined some co-workers in a trendy district. We entered a club that reminded me of a tacky perfume commercial. White leather seats, fur carpets, and glass chandeliers adorned the interior.

After an hour, we switched to a different club filled with a sea of tables covered in colored lights and whiskey glasses. We grabbed a table with bottle service while Harold Frost, a guy from the office, told jokes. When the discussion shifted from office politics to local prostitution, I got up to dance. It wasn't long before I started receiving text messages.

Daniel:	*Hey Batman take a taxi to Huai Huai Lu cross the intersection walk a few blocks meet me in front of the 7-11 about a hundred feet around the corner*
Me:	*No thanks*
Daniel:	*Don't you want free booze?*
Me:	*Thanks, but we've got that*
Daniel:	*Your loss, this is a great house party*

I didn't bother to respond.

Daniel: Batman you win – I'll meet you

I left the dance floor to visit the restroom, which was down a dark corridor. When I returned, I stopped to recheck my makeup in the nightclub's mirrored walls.

As I leaned toward the mirror, I heard someone joke, "Are you trying to pee?"

"What?" I spun around and was surprised to see Daniel.

"Lana, c'mon, let's dance up here," he said, as he took my hand and pulled me up on to the stage, where we observed a group of drunken expats below.

"Do you think they've known each other for very long?" I asked while observing two couples, in opposite corners of the room, furiously making out.

Daniel shook his head, "Nope, they probably met tonight."

He then snapped a photo, posted it on Flickr and wrote, *True love in Shanghai.*

"They should get a room," I suggested.

"They won't be going home together," Daniel predicted.

"How do you know?"

"The women will break it off. That's when someone like me walks in and applies plausible deniability."

"Plausible deniability?"

"I'll say, 'Do you want to go back to my place and watch *The Lion King*? But of course we won't."

"Um, okay," I said skeptically.

"C'mon Batman, let's follow them, so I can prove I'm right."

Daniel helped me down, seized me by the waist and whispered, "Careful not to stare at them, keep your eyes focused on mine."

He then spun me around while giving me kisses on the cheek. We were turning around and around, dancing cheek-to-cheek while watching the strangers leave the club. We followed them as they headed to the street.

In the middle of our frolic, the two blonde women suddenly cut ties with their make out buddies, hailed a taxi, and jumped in. As the taxi sped away, the men looked puzzled.

I stopped dancing, walked a few steps to the side and said, "Gosh, you were right. What a strange encounter."

"Not really," Daniel remarked. "Now I have to take off unless you want to come home with me and watch *The Lion King*."

"Thanks, but I need to get home."

"Alright, Batman, your loss."

CHAPTER 10

The next morning, I was one of the few people in the office before 8 a.m. I drafted a letter for a client who sought to repudiate a contract with a supplier.

Harold startled me when he crept around the corner and whispered loudly, "Lana, what are you working on?"

"A client letter," I gasped with surprise.

"We all saw you dancing with that guy last night," teased Harold, a tall, heavy-set blonde from Minnesota.

"Uh, huh," I said.

"Lana, I almost didn't recognize you,"

"Why?"

"Your outfit. Normally, you dress like my granny."

"Your grandmother has good taste."

"She shops at garage sales," Harold confessed with a twinkle in his eye.

I sighed a deep breath and promised, "Next time I'm out, I'll give your phone number to the creepiest men I encounter."

"Mine? Give them Eric's." Harold joked while sauntering back to the IP department.

I tried to focus on reading a contract, but was distracted

by a text: *Hey Batman, wassup!*

I wrote back: *You're up early.*

He responded: *I never went to bed!!*

Super busy, we'll talk later, I replied, because I realized that the office staff was staring at me. I worried they'd say I spent too much time texting.

CHAPTER 11

Cindy wasn't impressed by Paul's opinions, so a week after talking to him she went to a networking event knowing Lana would be there. As she walked into a French restaurant filled with cigarette smoke, she spotted a woman wearing a white suit.

A tall Belgian had cornered her and asserted, "That Shanghainese 'know-it-all,' over there, knows nothing."

"What do you mean?" Lana asked innocently.

"Well, Wong keeps saying that having money in Shanghai doesn't guarantee deals."

"I see."

"He insists that having money isn't as important as relationships."

"Ah, okay," Lana conceded.

"Sure, China is all about relationships, but people with money have connections."

"You know a lot about China. What do you do?"

William replied, "I was trained as a lawyer, but I now run a hedge fund out of Argentina. I'm here to make contacts with wealthy Chinese people who want to invest in Latin American projects."

Lana responded, "You don't think Wong has valuable insight into his own country?"

"Not at all," William flippantly declared as he headed towards the bar for more whiskey.

Within seconds, Cindy saw another guy approach Lana.

"Good job, Lana," Harold said sarcastically.

"What are you talking about?"

"You just pissed off that Belgian lawyer."

"Why do you say that?"

"You're so smarmy."

"What does that mean?"

"Insincere."

"I've been called worse."

"You smile when you talk." Harold mimicked Lana's mannerisms.

"Then why are you always talking to me?"

"You're talking to me."

"Not by choice," Lana protested.

"Why don't you own up to why you come to these events," Harold demanded.

"It's part of the job."

"Admit it. You're on the prowl, desperately hunting for fresh man meat."

"I need to go, I have to find my friend," Lana said.

Harold slapped her on the back and shouted, "Lana, your friend is fat, and you're a bad dancer."

Lana looked hurt by what was likely intended to be a playful slap. Upset, she doused Harold with her cup of water and exclaimed, "How dare you touch me!"

That's when Cindy decided to intervene. Running up to Lana, she grabbed her by the waist and said, "C'mon Lana, our friends are waiting for us. Let's go because we're late."

Lana looked confused but allowed Cindy to pull her away from Harold. His hair and shirt were wet. Water rolled off of his baffled face.

Lana asked, "How do you know my name?"

"Your name tag," Cindy said, pointing to Lana's chest.

"Oh, I completely forgot," Lana said sheepishly. She removed the sticker and tossed it in a bin.

"My name is Cindy."

"Thanks for your help."

"Who is he?"

"A guy I work with," Lana explained.

"Next time you get into a row, don't throw water in his face."

Lana reacted as if she had been reprimanded and asked, defensively, "Why?"

"Because he might hit you back," Cindy exclaimed.

Lana nodded.

"My friends have a table at a club, next door, where a live band is playing. Do you want to join?"

"Sure," Lana said as she followed Cindy. "You have such a beautiful British accent. You must be from —"

"Hong Kong, but I went to a British boarding school," Cindy responded.

"Gosh, you must have missed your family."

"Yeah, it was hard," Cindy said curtly while walking up a flight of stairs to the nightclub where music was blasting loudly.

"I bet. I'm very close to my mother," Lana babbled nervously.

"Lana, I want you to meet my best friend Amy. She's almost as sweet as you."

CHAPTER 12

A few weeks later, Lana and Cindy sat at an outdoor café in Shanghai's historic *French Concession*. Since meeting, the two had seen each other three to four times a week. Lana enjoyed having friends like Amy and Cindy: outgoing, professional women with enviable careers.

Cindy gently sipped tea and nibbled a pastry, while Lana ravenously gulped coffee and wolfed down a sandwich.

"How was your event the other night?"

Lana shrugged. "Okay. Typical, like the one we were at a few weeks ago."

"Does your company pay?"

"Never, which is tough because I'm up to my ears in debt."

Cindy nodded.

"Besides, I meet better people in less contrived situations."

Cindy abruptly changed the subject. "Lana, I know you don't have a boyfriend —"

"Nope, no boyfriend."

"What about that guy you mentioned last week?"

"Daniel?" Lana laughed, "He doesn't count."

"Why not?"

"He's a screwball and a player."

"I bet you're holding a torch for someone from school, right?"

"Not at all, why on earth would you think that?"

"So what's your type?"

Lana sighed and said, "I don't have one."

"C'mon, everyone has a type."

Lana thought for a second and then declared, "Folks who give me plenty of space."

"Are you serious?"

"Yep, I'm very independent."

"That's not good," Cindy responded.

"Why?"

"Because men like to be in charge and want someone who is nurturing."

Lana shrugged and said flippantly, "That's not my problem."

"So you wear the pants in relationships!" Cindy exclaimed.

"Yep, it's my way or the highway."

Cindy laughed. "You sound like a feminist."

"I don't like labels."

Cindy nodded and said, "Feminism aside, I love cooking, especially for my boyfriend. You and Amy should come over sometime for dinner, soon."

Lana smiled appreciatively and to be polite said, "I heard Amy mention you've got a boyfriend in Hong Kong."

"Yes," Cindy responded enthusiastically, "but our relationship is complicated."

"Cool, at least it's not boring," Lana remarked, but she now looked very bored.

CHAPTER 13

After meeting Lana for coffee, Cindy returned to work, but first stopped by her best friend's office. Amy Liu was a tall, slender woman from Beijing. She had distinctive features such as a square jaw, full lips, and eyes like a doll.

As she knocked on the door, Cindy asked, "Hi Amy, how's that report coming along?"

"Good, it's almost ready. How was lunch with Lana?"

"Fine. It's hard to dislike her completely."

"Yes, I agree," Amy replied as she looked up from her paperwork.

"Lana is very easy to talk to."

"Cindy, I think you should be careful," her friend warned.

"Why?"

"You might say too much."

"I've asked lots of questions, but Lana hasn't mentioned Curt — not even once."

"Uh, huh."

"She may not know that he even exists."

Amy exhaled and said, "So what? Was that ever the issue?"

"Lana is not Curt's type," Cindy declared firmly.

"Are you sure about that?"

"Yeah, she's too strong."

"And you're not?" Amy teased.

"I am, but I know how to hide my claws."

"Uh, huh, well, you certainly know Steiger, I'll agree to that."

Cindy continued, "Lana is way too combative with men."

Amy agreed, "She's quite direct."

"Yep, she's too genuine and lacks basic survival skills."

"Lana is young, she'll adapt."

Cindy shook her head. "Maybe guys find her fun to debate. However, no man especially, Curt Steiger, wants to put up with that for very long."

Amy yawned and said, "In some ways, she's kind of like him."

"Well, Lana is a prima donna, if that's what you mean."

CHAPTER 14
August 2009
Lana Hayaak

It was my last Friday in Shanghai. By next Thursday, I would return to the Bay Area and finish my final year of law school. I was ambivalent. There were things I would miss about Shanghai: the nightlife and the diversity; however, I was anxious to return home.

I was supposed to meet up with Cindy, Amy, and Gwen for dinner at a Japanese restaurant in the *French Concession*. I hadn't told them I was leaving soon because I didn't want things to be awkward. As much as I liked the girls, I wondered if the feeling was mutual.

I admired Cindy because she was sophisticated, but at times her jokes were brazen. It often seemed as if she was lashing out, but I wasn't entirely sure. For example, last Sunday I wanted to finish reviewing documents at a coffee shop, but:

The girls showed up at my apartment and invited me to an outdoor bar full of men watching sports. I was uncomfortable while studying a menu devoid of vegetarian options.

Cindy was eager to learn about a recent date. Reluctantly I explained, "It was awful. I met the French guy for wine, but within five minutes, he leaned in to say "Lana, you'll make a bad lawyer." Then he complained about Americans. So I got up and stormed out, but he kept texting me."

In response, Cindy complained, "Lana, why do your dates always end in conflict? I don't think I've ever fought with a date."

Amy and Gwen said nothing. I felt attacked and regretted sharing, so I got up and headed to the coffee shop. An hour later, Cindy popped up to grill me about a different encounter. Then she took off, leaving me with her unpaid bill.

I looked at my watch and realized I would have to hurry if I wanted to arrive at dinner on time. I quickly showered and put on a silky green dress with a draping neckline.

When I entered the restaurant, I felt people peering in my direction. I glanced around but didn't see my friends. So I ran up the stairs and saw them at a table in the back.

"I'm sorry I'm late," I apologized.

"No worries, I got your texts," Cindy reassured me.

"Hi Gwen," I said to a tall Swedish girl who was only nineteen but looked mature for her age. She was a ravishing blonde; everywhere we went people stared. Chinese tourists often stopped and asked me to take their picture with her.

"Lana, earth to Lana," Cindy teased as she had caught me daydreaming.

"Huh?" I asked.

"Lana, the waitress wants your drink order," Amy said.

"A Manhattan," I replied.

"I hate it when men tell me I'm beautiful or that I have a good body," Gwen complained.

"Must be nice," I grumbled with my nose in the menu.

"What was that, Lana?" Amy asked.

"Gwen is lucky. Men just invade my space to make coarse remarks."

"Oh, poor Lana," Cindy taunted. I didn't appreciate her

mockery and felt slighted. After all, I wasn't looking for validation. What was I supposed to do, brag like Gwen?

I ordered my food and went to the ladies' room because I was already feeling anti-social.

When I returned, a pack of sleazy men was at our table. Within minutes, their leader ran downstairs with Gwen. Cindy giggled as the other guys asked us to join them. I rejected the plan.

"C'mon Lana, this could be fun," Cindy urged.

I disagreed, but finally gave in and moved with Amy and Cindy to the other table. I took my Manhattan and sat down next to a guy named Jim who was yelling at the staff.

"Hey, I don't want this, take it back," Jim demanded, as he shoved a platter of sushi at the server.

The Chinese waiter looked stressed. I had seen these guys order a lot and knew that this particular entrée was theirs. *Who orders sushi and sends it back?*

Meanwhile, Cindy and Amy accepted cocktails from them.

I asked, "So what brings you to Shanghai?"

"We're only here for the weekend," Jim explained. "It's Ryan's bachelor party."

Well, this is another group of real winners, I thought sarcastically. I watched Gwen return from her romp downstairs. Her hair, blouse, and lipstick were a mess. Ryan had lipstick stains around his mouth.

Before I could finish eating, Cindy and Ryan decided we should head to the nightclub ahead of the other guys. I didn't feel like eating with Jim and his friends, so I reluctantly followed.

During the taxi ride and before arriving at our destination, Ryan turned to me and said, "Are you Chinese?"

"Lana is not Chinese. She looks American," Gwen volunteered.

"Nah, she looks Chinese," Ryan insisted.

"I'm American," I said tersely.

"Nah, you're not white," Ryan retorted.

"Never said I was," I responded with irritation.

Gwen interjected, "Only her eyes are slightly Asian."

"Hey, we're here, get out!" Cindy said.

I started to pull out some money, but Gwen and Cindy insisted I put it away.

"Let him pay," Cindy hissed.

"Fine" I said, not caring.

The five of us stopped by the club entrance to check-in. Cindy, Amy, Gwen, and I were already on the guest list, so we didn't have to pay the outrageous cover charge. Meanwhile, Ryan didn't have a reservation, so he unsuccessfully attempted to bluff his way past the gatekeepers.

We eventually entered the club, located on the top floor. I immediately snuck off to the ladies' room. When I returned, the girls were drinking champagne that Ryan had bought for them. They smiled and laughed at his tasteless jokes, but no one offered me anything to drink.

Abruptly and unexpectedly, Ryan seized my wrist and forced me on to the dance floor. He put his hands on my hips and authoritatively ordered me to dance faster and sexier. Repulsed, I immediately shoved him with all of my strength and pulled away.

Cindy rushed up and said, "Hey Lana, relax! Ryan is after Gwen, not you, so just relax!"

I was sick and tired of people telling me what to do, so I abandoned the group and stormed off. I could hear Ryan loudly complaining about me.

As I jumped into the elevator, I got texts from Cindy: *Hey, where are you going?*

I ignored her texts and hit ground floor.

When I got outside, I ran to the curb and hailed a taxi. I didn't feel like going home, so I headed to a club nearby on the Bund. When I arrived, the place was already crowded.

I stood in a less congested area and saw someone who looked familiar. He approached and asked, "So are you going to dance on the stage?"

"We've met, haven't we?"

"Yeah, Lana, we've already met.," he replied with scorn in his light colored eyes.

I nodded and said, "Of course, I remember. Sorry, how do you pronounce your name again?"

"Yeah, I hear that a lot because Paul is a tough name to pronounce."

I didn't respond and attempted a weak — albeit fake — smile.

Paul then asked, "Who are your friends?"

"A variety of people," I replied, but impatiently wondered why people always ask such dumb questions. *Why does anyone, including this stranger, care whom I'm friends with? Is this junior high?*

"Sure," Paul said with disbelief. "You know it's dangerous for a woman like you to be out alone."

I wanted to say: *Does this faux-daddy speech work on anyone?* But I was drained, so I asserted, "Actually, it's more dangerous when I'm out with groups."

"Why's that?" Paul asked with a raised eyebrow.

"When I go out with other women, we attract jerks and I get attacked which creates a rift with my girlfriends."

"Aw, poor girl," Paul mocked.

"I have to go," I mumbled and turned to walk away. I regretted talking to this person.

I waded through the manic crowd and climbed up on to the stage. Soon I was dancing with friendly people and my spirits dramatically improved. But then I started receiving texts.

Cindy wrote: *OMG Lana. I can't believe you left. We went back to Ryan's hotel. There's cocaine!*

Good idea, I thought sarcastically, *When in China, take illegal drugs.* When we lived in KL, my parents discussed drugs frequently because Southeast Asia was fertile territory for contraband. In Malaysia, there was a saying *"da da is death."*

I wondered if Ryan and his friends even had cocaine. I figured these clowns were trying to impress my girlfriends. In any event, it was the last thing I needed, since I still hadn't finished my moral character application required by the State Bar of California.

I texted back: *I'm too busy with my game of Russian Roulette.* After all, taking narcotics in China was as reasonable as playing with a loaded gun.

I talked to people nearby and regularly checked texts from Cindy, which were growing increasingly erratic, evidently due to substance use. She seemed determined to involve me in her hedonistic games.

I continued dancing and tried to forget about Cindy and Ryan who had triggered memories of high school and college in Oregon, where drug use was prevalent. While living in the house in Portland, I had continued my investigation into my parents' background. I had no physical evidence and had to rely on past conversations. When Mom and Dad thought I was asleep, they spent an inordinate amount of time discussing drugs in Southeast Asia.

The club's volume increased as the crowds swelled. I felt a throbbing headache because even in Shanghai, at a nightclub, my thoughts were a million miles away and thirty thousand feet off the ground.

CHAPTER 15

In the corner of the nightclub, an athletic, ethnically ambiguous man named Aaron Walker entertained a group of clients at his private table. He approached a security guard and asked, "What can you tell me about that woman?"

"The one in the green dress?" asked Jakov Horvat, a very tall Slav from Croatia. A lot of clubs in Shanghai contracted with security companies that hired guards from places such as the Balkans.

"Yeah."

"Just another student here for the summer," Jakov responded.

"Okay, thanks."

"Return tomorrow," the security guard suggested.

"Why?" Aaron asked.

"Saturday is EDM night. She'll be here."

"Okay, thanks for the information."

CHAPTER 16
Lana Hayaak

The next evening, I sought to avoid a repeat of last night's fiasco, which meant avoiding any private parties. *I have a better time when I'm alone*, I thought as I dashed into the street to hail a taxi. Traffic had finally cleared, the air was warm, and raindrops fell occasionally from the black sky.

I had a late dinner in *Xintiandi*, which was unusually quiet for a Saturday. So I went to the *Bund*, but when I entered the club by the riverside, I discovered that it was equally vacant.

I spotted Paul and noticed that he was in an upbeat mood. He strolled up and hugged me like we were lifelong companions.

"Lana, that man over on the terrace was here last night and dropped more than 2,000 dollars on drinks for his friends."

"Am I supposed to be impressed?" I asked in a somewhat haughty manner.

"Hey, what's with the attitude?"

I shrugged. "We were out with a guy last night who was throwing money around and he practically assaulted me."

"You're so dramatic," Paul said while rolling his eyes.

"Ryan grabbed my wrists and forced me to dance."

"Lana, you were at a fucking nightclub, what the hell do you expect?"

"Doesn't matter," I replied curtly.

"Anyway, Aaron is a great guy, so I bought him dinner," Paul continued.

"Sounds like a date," I taunted.

"Hey!" Paul protested, "I value good customers."

"Sure," I teased.

"Just now while you were getting a drink, Aaron pulled me over and was asking about you."

"Uh, huh," I murmured with disinterest. I directed my eyes towards the door to see who else had arrived.

"He kept asking if you're a lesbian," Paul declared abruptly.

"What an impertinent question," I stammered indignantly. "What did you say?"

"I said, 'her type usually is,' but Aaron said, 'nah, she's too pretty to be gay.'"

"Please don't involve me in your sordid affairs."

"Fuck you, Lana," Paul snarled.

"Aren't you the gentleman," I quipped.

I started to depart when the man, whom Paul pointed out, strode up to me. From far away, I had noted that Aaron was tall and Asiatic. However, I now realized he was at least six foot four and extremely muscular, yet lean like a Navy Seal. He was definitely Eurasian, and if I had to guess, he was probably half German and half Korean.

I never saw men like this back home in Silicon Valley, at least not in law school. I peeked past Aaron and saw Paul scampering off, like a displaced hyena. Vexation had replaced his formerly cheerful mood.

"Can I buy you a drink?" Aaron asked.

I blurted, "I don't think that was a very nice question."

"Sorry, I didn't intend to offend you," he apologized.

"I see, well you're completely entitled to your opinions, but don't you think your presumption was misogynistic?"

"Asking if I can buy you a drink?" Aaron asked with confusion. "Geez, American women are complicated."

"Unbelievable," I stammered, "First you assume that only unattractive women can be gay and now you generalize nationalities."

"Whoa, what are you talking about?" Aaron demanded. In the distance, I could see Paul smirking, while imitating my passionate declarations.

Stridently, I continued, "Paul said that you asked if I'm a lesbian, but then determined I'm too attractive to be gay."

Aaron stared at me blankly, so I continued my lecture. "For your information, countless beautiful women have been homosexual, and for you to assume otherwise is sexist because no one would say that about a gay man."

"I didn't say anything like that —"

"Paul told me you did."

"Lana, I never asked if you were a lesbian," Aaron asserted.

"I see," I said with skepticism. "How do you know my name?"

"Your friend, if you can call him that, told me."

"Oh," I said, calming down a bit.

Aaron continued, "All I asked was is she Asian."

I glanced into his hazel eyes because the exotic mixture of green and brown reminded me of my own. It was almost like staring into a mirror and seeing a male version of myself.

Finally, I looked away, but conceded, "I guess there's been a misunderstanding." I glared at Paul who was now sauntering about like an amused jackal. I wanted to strangle him.

Aaron smiled and said, "I was here last night with a group of clients, but left around 1 a.m."

I nodded. "Yesterday, I was at another club with friends,

but left."

"Why?"

"My friends met a pack of guys who wanted to do cocaine."

"Sounds like you need new friends," Aaron suggested.

"Thank you, but I'm fine on my own," I responded indignantly.

"Everyone needs friends."

I looked down to check my messages from Cindy: *Lana where are you? Are you at that place filled with weirdos? Why do you go there?*

I didn't appreciate Cindy's judgmental remarks. After all, she favored dive bars filled with men and no dance floor. If I wanted to hang out exclusively with guys, then I had plenty of opportunities for that back home. After all, Silicon Valley had almost as many women as a men's prison.

I preferred clubs that attracted beautiful women from countries such as Ukraine, Kazakhstan, and Azerbaijan. Sometimes I couldn't figure out if they were White or Asian.

One night, I met a stunning Russian woman named Ludmilla. After chatting, I discovered that her father was with the Russian embassy and had grown up attending Chinese schools. She was charming, culturally astute, and fluent in Mandarin.

I was impressed that Russian diplomats sent their children to local schools because it saved their tax-payers money and allowed for complete cultural immersion.

I looked back at Aaron and said, "My friends want to meet up for karaoke."

He grinned. "So, do you want to go to KTV or stay here with me?"

I hesitated because I wasn't sure, but when I looked across the room I saw Paul giving me the middle finger and mouthing obscenities. I sighed and thought, *Two years of law school didn't prepare me for interacting with adults who hadn't evolved past the third grade.*

Finally, I turned back to Aaron and confessed, "I can't sing."

"Then let's dance," he said.

***

Aaron and I were dancing on the empty dance floor when my girlfriends arrived. Cindy, Amy, and Gwen spotted my new acquaintance and approached with curiosity. After brief introductions, Aaron headed to the bar and ordered drinks for everyone.

"Lana, why did you leave last night?" asked Cindy who was wearing a fashionable bandage dress.

"I didn't feel comfortable," I confessed. "Did you have fun?"

"Yes," Gwen exclaimed. "I left with Ryan, but we didn't have sex."

"How romantic," I quipped.

"Yeah, we tried, but he couldn't because of the cocaine," she continued.

Gwen's candor was typical of her generation. Her authenticity was very Scandinavian.

I responded dryly, "Shocking … performance issues from someone so cocky."

Gwen laughed. "C'mon Lana, Ryan was nice. The next day he even bought me a Prada bag."

"You missed out," Amy teased me.

"Apparently," I agreed as Aaron returned with our drinks.

The club was now packed and impossible to move within.

"Lana, why don't we head to the club across the street?" Cindy suggested. She seemed annoyed by something, because she barked orders at Gwen and Amy.

"Sure," I agreed.

"You and your friend can go ahead of us," she

continued. "We're waiting for other friends to join us."

Aaron was too tall to hear me, so he leaned down so I could explain our new game plan.

As we exited and ventured outside he remarked, "I love the outdoors, don't you?"

"I'm more of an indoor kind of girl," I confessed.

"I'd never guess," Aaron joked while appreciating my attire.

I was wearing a short ultra-feminine dress. The bodice was strapless but shaped like a heart and tapered at the waist. Lace peeked from the bottom of my puffy skirt, which was white, but covered in a floral pattern. I wore high heels that looked like glass slippers while carrying a sequined clutch bag and a see-through lavender colored scarf.

"You need a tan," Aaron suggested.

"I don't get out much," I explained, which was true. I spent most of my time in the office, class, or the library. I was like one of the cave dwellers in H.G. Well's *Time Machine*.

"Do you hunt or fish?"

"Never," I replied. I thought Aaron's question was unusual since we were in Shanghai. In Wyoming or Texas, it might be more appropriate.

"That's too bad because it's a lot of fun."

Killing animals is fun? Changing the subject, I said, "If I had a brother, I bet he'd look like you."

"Your brother?" Aaron asked with astonishment. "You think I look like your brother?"

"Sure."

I wondered if Aaron was like the Eurasian criminal in the case I read for Con Law: *Nguyen v. Texas.*

We were now walking up the steps to a different nightclub.

"Lana, do you know why I like you?"

"My personality," I said unequivocally.

"It's because we're complete opposites."

"Uh, huh," I murmured.

"In an apocalypse, you'd need me."

"Thanks, but I can take care of myself."

"Nah, you can't fish or hunt."

While Aaron bragged, my mind wandered.

FLASHBACK 1995

My parents were in the dining room and didn't know that I was eavesdropping. It was past midnight, and I was supposed to be asleep. Mom and Dad were at their cherry-wood dining table counting large sums of money. The Casablanca fan purred, but I heard:

"Jason, I was thinking of teaching Natalia archery."

"Why?"

"I'm highly skilled at it."

"Waste of time. I bought our daughter a computer for a reason."

"It's proven to be an expensive paper weight."

"Lara, the future is in Silicon Valley."

"Jason, our daughter is a girly girl. She's not cut out for the tech industry."

"Lana?" Aaron repeated.

I struggled to catch my breath. "What did you say?"

"If you were in the Middle East, who would be more useful?"

"Why would I be in the Middle East?" I slurred. I felt sick from the alcohol.

"Me or them?" Aaron asked as he glanced at a group of suits standing by the bar. I recognized a few from networking events.

"What?" I was disoriented, but alert enough to realize that this perfectly chiseled stranger was way too contrived.

"Me," Aaron boasted.

Who talks like this? Suddenly I saw Cindy, Amy, and Gwen march into the club.

Maybe it was the alcohol, but something was off. My

heart was racing and my palms were sweaty. I felt anxious and wanted to leave immediately. Who were these people? Why were they in my life?

PART 3
2013

CHAPTER 1

San Francisco
Lana Hayaak

I dreaded seeing the dentist, even for routine cleanings. I had an incredibly high tolerance for pain, but was wary of bad news since there had been plenty in the past.

My problems developed in my teens while living in Portland. I didn't have medical insurance, so I never saw a doctor and skipped dental exams during my first year in Oregon. An untreated cavity grew into a root canal, later a second root canal, and most recently, a dental implant. Seeing a new dentist always made me especially nervous.

As I lay uncomfortably in this new dentist's chair, a large, heavy-set doctor grinned as he sadistically leaned in to analyze my teeth. He then laughed and said, "Lana, I know everything about you by just looking at you."

"I beg your pardon?"

"Was your dad very tall and your mom very short?"

"Not really."

"Yeah, but you're Eurasian, right?"

"Um, yes," I admitted.

"My mom was Eurasian. Her dad was very tall, and her

mom was very short," the dentist shared.

"Uh, huh."

"How did your parents meet?"

I couldn't believe this was happening. Dental visits were bad enough, but being questioned about my parents was like a bad dream. I took a deep breath and replied, "Dad tutored Mom in statistics."

He laughed and asked, "What kind of an Asian woman isn't good at math?"

"She's not Asian," I declared impatiently. "Can we please discuss my dental implant? I'm very concerned about it."

"Sure, but first let me tell you about my mother because I'm sure you'll relate."

"What?" I asked. I felt trapped and wondered if this doctor was insane.

The dentist blabbered, "She was born in the Philippines and grew up in an orphanage."

"How can I relate to this?" I demanded, while the overbearing man pressed up against me.

"I can see you've had a hard life."

"Excuse me?"

"Well, you've obviously got a stressful one, because you grind your teeth a lot."

"I wear a night guard, but yeah … how many people my age have a dental implant?"

"What do you do for fun?"

"Mop the kitchen floor." I was relieved by the subject shift because I didn't like discussing Mom and Dad.

The doctor was still jabbering: "Your teeth are super stained. You must drink a lot of coffee."

"One cup a day is less than average."

"You must be the woman in the slow lane!"

I didn't say anything, but clenched my hands.

"Lana, I can read body language. You need to be more artful with your hands."

"Why? Is this a ballet recital?"

When my dental appointment was finally over, I left in a lousy mood. Was my headache due to the dentist's scalpel or his drilling into my past?

As I scurried down Market Street, I felt as if someone was following me. Meanwhile a stranger yelled, "Hey lady, smile!"

I ran down the stairs into the BART Station.

"Lana, hey wait up," shouted a familiar voice. I looked up and realized it was my former classmate. Curt had gained weight but looked the same. He still had his perfect smile. I bet dentists loved him and never gave him grief.

Ignoring him, I rifled through my purse, pulled out a credit card and struggled to purchase a ticket.

"Lana, don't you recognize me?" Curt asked.

"Sure," I grumbled as I brushed past him and headed down the escalators to the tracks.

"I haven't seen you in years. Do you want to grab a bite?"

"Why?"

"We're friends?" Curt replied.

"Not exactly," I clarified.

I jumped into a subway car and took a seat, but he sidled up to me and asked, "Don't you think you're overly sensitive about what I said years ago?"

"Stop labeling me," I demanded while hopping up to move.

Curt pursued me and said, "I'm having a party this weekend —"

"I can't," I lied.

"Why?"

"I don't like you."

"Let's end this game of cat and mouse. You're too old for games."

I headed towards the exit doors. Curt pushed his way through a horde of exhausted San Franciscans to stand near me. He whispered loudly, "I think you're jealous of Cindy."

People were now staring. I wanted to leave, but there was no place to go.

I shook my head and said, "I never knew Cindy was your girlfriend, but then I saw her posts on Facebook."

Curt laughed and said, "It was a coincidence."

Impatiently I exclaimed, "There's no such thing."

"Guess what Lana, the world isn't as cold and calculating as you imagine."

"Please go away," I murmured.

"I met Cindy when I was getting my PhD."

"So, what?"

"We broke up, so maybe we can hang out sometime."

"Nope, buh-bye," I quipped as the doors opened and I bounced off.

While the doors shut on Curt's face, an old bum with a gray beard said, "Dude, she's just not into you."

CHAPTER 2
San Francisco

The next day, I walked rapidly down California Street. I opened my purse to find some aspirin while a homeless man tumbled into me. Startled, I darted into the middle of oncoming traffic and narrowly avoided being hit by a car.

I dashed over to the side of the street and a young Asian street sweeper asked, "Are you okay, miss?"

I smiled at him appreciatively and said, "I'm fine, thank you."

I wandered around the corner and took a seat at a popular Irish bar. While reading the menu, I saw a beautiful woman with an hourglass figure and long brown hair enter the restaurant. I ran up to give her a big hug and said, "Maria, it's so good to see you."

She hugged me back and exclaimed, "Lana, it's been ages."

"Has it? The last four years flew by."

"What have you been doing?"

"I took a marketing job."

"Where?" Maria asked with interest.

"East Coast," I replied.

"Cool, which city?"

"The company is incorporated in Delaware, but has offices all over the world."

"Yes, but where were you based?"

"Outside of D.C., but I was on the road so much. There were offices in Boston," I explained.

Maria nodded. "So you completely left the law?"

"I don't think we can ever really leave, can we?"

"What do you mean?" Maria practiced M&A law at a prestigious firm.

"Nothing," I replied, "How's your sister?"

CHAPTER 3
Mountain View, CA

On Saturday, a few days after seeing Maria, I ventured out of my apartment and headed towards downtown Mountain View. It was sunny, yet windy, so I struggled to keep my hat from flying off my head.

I had a lot on my mind. While waiting for the train to pass I thought about rent, which had recently increased. I also thought about offensive messages I had been receiving from a guy I knew in high school. While caught in thought, Curt ran up to me.

"Are you stalking me?" I demanded.

"Sort of, I know you like this area," he replied.

"How?"

"Your online Yelp reviews."

"You need a life," I suggested.

"You wouldn't return my calls."

"Take the hint."

"You should use a fake name if you want anonymity," Curt advised.

"You're so bossy," I complained.

"Yep, I'm now a boss," he said proudly.

I ignored Curt and slipped into a café.

While standing in line he asked, "How's work?"

I sighed and decided to be more agreeable. "It's okay. But I need a new apartment and a new job."

"Why didn't you return to that law firm in Shanghai?"

"It closed after the recession hit China. Their workload depended upon import-export accounts."

I was now at the counter and put in an order for an Americano. Before I could pay, Curt intervened and handed the barista money.

"You seemed to love it over there," Curt remarked.

"Sure," I admitted while grabbing a seat at a table by the window. "I'm a Luddite, so it suited me."

"You're a Luddite?" he scoffed while sitting down next to me.

"Yes," I replied.

"Actions speak louder than words."

"What's that supposed to mean?"

"You constantly complain about Silicon Valley and its machismo culture, yet here you are."

"I'm surprised you know what a Luddite is," I said while silently wondering if he knew its link to the 19th century poet Lord Byron, who had stormed into the House of Lords defending the rights of the working classes against the onslaught of industrialization.

"Yep, I'm not the unlettered troglodyte that you think I am," Curt said with a smug grin.

"Is that so?" I teased while raising an eyebrow.

"Did you know that Lord Byron's daughter Ada Lovelace was the first computer programmer?" Curt asked. Instantly, I regretted encouraging him.

"Yes, of course I know that … who doesn't?" I said defensively, but I was bluffing because I had no idea what he was talking about.

Curt laughed. "If you started a Luddite club, who would build your platform?"

I shrugged indifferently. "I'd hire someone."

"Yep, a software engineer."

"Fine, if it makes you happy, I'll admit that tech guys *occasionally* have a purpose."

"Would you want to return to China?" Curt suddenly asked. The question surprised me, because it was such an abrupt change in the conversation.

"I guess?"

"I'm moving to Shanghai to set up new pharmaceutical labs."

"How nice for you," I said with a pang of jealousy.

"Would you want to go?"

"Why?"

"You don't have much here, do you?"

"Actually, I have a lot going on. I need to go," I said jumping up.

"What's the hurry?"

"I have to meet a couple of friends," I replied. This wasn't entirely a lie: Libby and Larry were a couple of stray cats I regularly fed. It was now past their feeding time.

Curt looked surprised, but he said almost apologetically, "Oh, okay, I didn't realize you had plans."

"Yep, thanks for the coffee, but I can't keep Libby and Larry waiting. They're almost as busy as I am."

As I took off, I heard Curt mutter, "Larry? Who is Larry?"

PART 4
SHANGHAI

CHAPTER 1
2015
Lana Hayaak

August was an especially hot month in Shanghai. Curt and I had been married and living in China for over a year.

At first, I was wary of Curt's affection, because it was so unreal. However, he eventually wore me down. Only his father and some of our closest friends attended a small ceremony in Chicago. Curt's mother had died of cancer in 2012.

Marriage initially provided me with security, because I no longer had to worry about money. However, it also imposed a variety of restrictions and expectations that I found incredibly stressful.

Where we lived was an oasis within the stressful city. I was practically within walking distance of a tranquil Buddhist Temple that dated back to the 7th century. But I was also steps away from millions of people fiercely pursuing their livelihood.

I frequently visited the empty health club on the top floor of our service apartment complex's main building. The elevators had glass windows that showcased the city.

The attendants, like the concierge, were aloof yet pleasant.

Most days I climbed up a flight of marble steps and hung out by the pool on the rooftop. I tried to read, but my thoughts frequently turned to the past:

FLASHBACK 1989

Sitting outside my parents' bedroom, where the door was slightly ajar, I heard the following:

"Lara, why does our daughter have an ex-military sergeant for a teacher?"

"She needs discipline," Mom responded.

"Natalia is five."

"She draws flowers all over her homework."

Dad asked, "So she can't color in the lines?"

"Nope."

"When did that ever help us?"

"Jason, people need to follow the rules."

CHAPTER 2

I went shopping to find a new cocktail dress for parties we frequented. When I got home, the door to Curt's office was slightly ajar, and I could hear him on the phone. I knew I shouldn't listen because work discussions were confidential. However, I couldn't resist learning more.

My husband was always vague about work. My understanding of his company was limited to the following:

Curt was a pharmaceutical chemist but simultaneously served as General Counsel for a small American company that couldn't facilitate its drug testing in the US. Thus, this cancer research company had outsourced drug development to Shanghai, China. The development site could perform all preclinical tests. Most of the time, his work pertained more to chemistry than the law.

I leaned in to listen, but abruptly Curt swung the door wide open, and I practically fell to the floor.

"Hold on a second," Curt said to the person on the phone. "I'll have to call you back."

"Hi Curt," I stammered nervously hoping my husband wouldn't berate me for eavesdropping.

"Lana, I had no idea you were home. How long have you been here?"

"Not long. I just walked through the door," I lied while trying to regain my composure.

Curt nodded. "Did you research the details of our trip to *Xi'an*?"

"Um … I've been busy."

"Busy, doing what?"

"How difficult can *Xi'an* be? We can wing it."

"Woman, I'm going to kill you. Do I look like a man who wings it?"

"No, but you should try."

"Lana, our holiday requires a detailed list of sites, maps, directions, and everything else."

"Uh, huh," I murmured with disinterest.

"I'm very busy with work and rely on you to complete these details."

"Speaking of work, do you think it's a good idea to include non-competition and penalty clauses in your employment contracts?"

Curt stopped suddenly and asked, "Why were you reading through confidential documents?"

"You accidentally left them on the breakfast table," I replied nervously.

"I need to pack," Curt grumbled as he walked into the bedroom. "We don't have much time."

I shrugged casually. "It's not like we're going to *Pudong*. *Hongqiao* Airport isn't very far away."

"It's Friday night and traffic is always bad at this hour."

"Curt, I know you think those clauses are good deterrence practices. However, if you litigate in California then they might backfire."

"Can we talk about this later?"

"A California court could invalidate your entire contract which would affect the ownership of your scientists' work," I continued.

"Damn it," Curt screamed from the bedroom. "What the hell is this?"

"What is what?" I asked as I walked into our bedroom.

"This," Curt yelled pointing at his shoes covered in vomit.

"I didn't do it," I said holding my hands in the air like a criminal under arrest.

"No shit, Lana. I know you didn't throw up all over my shoes. Where is that bastard?"

"I'm so sorry, my darling," I said to Peter, my new friend who had captured my heart with his big green eyes, brick-pink nose, and black glove-like paws. He spent most of his time sunbathing behind the drapes by the window.

"Thank you, but I'm still angry."

"Curt, I wasn't talking to you. I was talking to Peter." I gently cradled my cat like a baby, while he swooned in my arms.

"I'm not sure which is more disgusting, this puke or the way you kiss that cat."

"I'm cleaning it up," I promised while running to get paper towels and Clorox wipes. "Maybe we should skip this trip since I don't want to leave Peter alone."

"No, the maids can take care of him."

"I wish we could take my little *bon vivant* with us."

"No, we're not taking him anywhere. Lana, please don't wear that hat."

"Why?"

"It's ridiculously huge. Do you want to be *that* person on the plane?"

CHAPTER 3

Curt sat in his office chair, facing the window, where he observed people walking along the streets of Shanghai's *Huai Huai Lu*. It was past 4 p.m., and he felt fatigued by the paperwork necessary to comply with the Chinese government's regulations. However, today his headaches had nothing to do with red tape.

Curt's partner and longtime friend, Ben, walked into his office and said, "Happy Birthday!"

Raised in Fremont, California, Ben Chang possessed high cheekbones, light skin, and a slender build. He wasn't very tall, yet his presence rivaled men twice his size.

"Thank you, Ben."

"Do you have plans?"

"Not really."

"I see."

"Cindy would have thrown a huge party for me," Curt grumbled.

Ben nodded. "Yes, she would have gone all out. What will your wife do this year?"

"I'll be lucky if she even remembers."

"Uh, huh."

"Lana barely knows our wedding anniversary."

"Maybe she'll see the Facebook alert?"

"Not likely, because she unfriended me on Facebook."

"Are you serious?"

"Yep, Lana said it's good for couples to have space."

Ben nodded without saying anything.

"She's the complete opposite of Cindy," Curt complained.

"How so?" Ben asked, pretending he didn't know the answer. However, he was well aware of the two women's differences.

"Cindy was very active on my Facebook page. She would tag me in photos, comment on posts, and question my female friendships."

"Uh, huh."

"Lana removed all photos of me. She didn't even post any wedding pictures, let alone update her relationship status to *married*."

"Your wife also kept her maiden name," Ben noted.

"Yep, she flatly refused to change it to Steiger."

"Isn't Hayaak a Middle Eastern surname? Is Lana Middle Eastern?"

"Nah, it's a long story."

Ben nodded.

Curt continued, "Cindy would have spent weeks planning something exceptional."

"It sounds like you miss Cindy. Do you?"

"Cindy was suffocating, but she was very attentive and loved cooking for me."

Ben nodded. "You can't want what you already have."

"Yeah, but Lana remains elusive."

"How so?"

"She's always preoccupied with things other than me."

"Are you referring to Lana's politics?"

"Yeah, she's the constant contrarian," Curt complained.

"What did Cindy like to do?"

"Cooking and shopping. I forget what else."

CHAPTER 4

Lana was at home studying maps of the *Silk Road* when she answered one of Curt's cell phones.

A man with a British accent asked, "May I please speak with Curt Steiger?"

"Sorry, he's not available," Lana responded brightly. "May I say who is calling?"

"Jon Eaton, I'm calling from Shark Global Investments. We assist expats with their finances."

"Alright Jon, I'll let him know you called."

As Lana hung up, she heard Curt barge into the bedroom.

"Who were you on the phone with?"

"Nobody," Lana said so abruptly that he immediately assumed she was talking to some guy.

Curt's eyes narrowed as he snapped impatiently, "Why aren't you dressed?"

"I am," Lana responded with surprise.

"Did you forget that it's my birthday?"

Flustered, Lana's face turned beet red as she dashed into the bedroom to change. Gasping to catch her breath she yelled, "Of course not."

"Yeah, right," Curt muttered sarcastically. "Alright, Lana, I'm going downstairs to review some documents. Buzz me when you're done."

Two hours later, the couple dined at a fashionable spot on the *Bund*.

While the waiter poured wine, Lana exclaimed, "I bought you a gift."

"Lana, this is quite unexpected," Curt said with astonishment. He was now hopeful that this year would better than the last.

"Yes, your birthday is your cat's adoption date. Don't you remember that Peter was your birthday present last year?"

"Yeah, I remember, and I think *that* cat was a gift to yourself. I hate cats," Curt complained while unwrapping his gift.

Lana said nothing as she took a sip of wine.

"You bought me a self-help book?"

"Yes, *How to Be a Better Cat Parent* has been on the Best Seller list for weeks."

"Thanks, I can't wait to read it," Curt said sarcastically.

"You're welcome, but that's not all."

"It's not?" Curt asked skeptically.

"Nope," Lana replied as she pulled out a receipt and handed it to her husband.

"This is a *Shanghai Tang* receipt. Did you buy me clothing?"

"I bought myself a new *qipao* dress. I know how much you like seeing me happy, so my birthday gift to you is a present for myself."

"Gee, thanks."

"You're welcome, Curt."

CHAPTER 5
Lana Hayaak

It was lunchtime as I sat with my friends Shelly and Gretchen at a *Sichuan* restaurant. It was a stylish locale adorned with dark wood paneling, *Ming Dynasty* seats, and moody red lighting.

Shelly was a British art teacher in her late thirties. Gretchen was an American doctor in her early forties, married to a finance manager.

"Shelly, I love your dress," I said.

"Thanks, Lana. I bought it at *People's Square* last Saturday."

"How's everything?" Gretchen asked both of us.

Shelly spoke while reading the menu, "Good, but it's tough dating a married man. However, I love his kids since they were students of mine."

I wasn't sure what to say.

Shelly continued, "I'm not in love with my boyfriend and always feel guilty after seeing him, but I can't resist his calls."

Gretchen said brusquely, "*That* guy is not your boyfriend. He's a married man with two kids."

"Well, this *is* Shanghai," Shelley reminded us.

"Come on, Shelley, how do you think Lana feels? She's married."

"Why? Is Curt fooling around?" Shelly asked.

"What an insensitive thing to say," Gretchen snapped.

"I didn't mean anything," Shelly insisted while hiding behind the menu.

The waiter returned and took our orders. It was only noon, but we ordered *Basiltinis* — martinis laced with lots of basil and sugar.

After the server left, I said, "It's alright Shelly. I know you didn't mean anything."

"Let's talk about something else," Gretchen insisted. "Lana, what type of research is your husband's company working on?"

"Cancer," I replied. "They're trying to develop a drug that would help the body's immune system combat illness."

"That's wonderful," Shelly exclaimed.

"I hope Curt succeeds," Gretchen said supportively.

"Thank you. If my husband achieves his goal, then the top 1% will never suffer cancer again."

"Lana, that's so cynical," Shelly remarked.

"It's realistic," I said flatly. "It's not as if these drugs will be affordable by the average person."

Gretchen responded, "Our healthcare system is a mess."

Shelly added, "We don't have your problems in the U.K."

The waiter had returned and filled the table with plates of steaming *Sichuan* entrees and bowls of rice.

I shrugged. "I wish Curt was trying to cure cancer out of the goodness of his heart. But he and his partner have a strong profit motive."

Shelly suddenly blurted, "There's been gossip about your husband's company."

"What are you talking about?" I asked with surprise.

"You haven't heard?" Shelly asked while trying to stifle a

nervous smile.

Gretchen looked impatient and said, "Lana, you should discuss this with Curt. C'mon Shelly, let's talk about events for our upcoming mixer."

Shelley laughed and said, "My tongue is numb from the spice. I can barely talk."

"We can only hope," Gretchen retorted.

I wondered what my friends were talking about, but I almost didn't want to know.

Curt and Ben were a cryptic pair. They were always sneaking around and whispering. I figured that they were obsessively trying to hide trade secrets from me. After all, if another company acquired their drug's intellectual property, then they wouldn't be able to create the monopoly they desperately sought.

CHAPTER 6

I fluttered around the apartment while Curt sat at his desk analyzing lab reports. Shanghai's morning sun poured through the glass balcony windows, while Peter was passed out like a drunk on his fake sheepskin bed, shaped like a doughnut.

"Curt, aren't you going into the office?"

"I'll go in later. First, I have a lot of paperwork to finish. I barely got any sleep thanks to *that* bastard."

"Don't call him that. Peter is my baby."

"That's the problem, you coddle him and he's a monster."

"Peter is the best thing that ever happened to me, so please leave him alone."

Curt snorted derisively and said, "That cat needs discipline, Lana."

"I don't believe in punishing something that lacks the *requisite mens rea* to form intent. Further, one doesn't own a cat. The cat owns us."

"The hell Peter owns me; I pay the bills. I'm king of this castle."

"A cat is the king of the jungle."

"Why do you let that rat walk all over our furniture?

I responded, "I respect the wild nature in the little beast, so I let him roam freely."

"I'm tired of seeing paw prints on the counters."

Changing the subject I asked, "What do you think of this outfit?"

Without glancing up Curt muttered, "It's fantastic. You should wear it."

"You didn't even look at me," I complained.

Finally shifting his eyes upwards, he remarked, "Your outfit is fine."

Peter was now awake, and kept brushing up against Curt.

I changed clothing and asked, "What about this one?"

"Isn't it a little much for an AmCham breakfast? Why are you going to this thing anyway?"

"Networking; I want to find a new job."

"You should write soap operas."

"I've never even seen one."

"But you've got a natural flair for high drama."

"Why not hire me at your company," I suggested.

"Never. You'd set the place on fire."

"Hey, that's not nice."

"C'mon, I've seen your cooking."

"What's wrong with my cooking?"

"Chemistry is like cooking; you need to be very precise."

"Recipes are like rules; they're meant to be broken."

Curt groaned, but as I headed towards the door he yelled, "Try not to get lost!"

"What's that supposed to mean?"

"You don't even know how to read a map."

***

I took off for the AmCham event. Bantering with Curt was a waste of precious time, because traffic was now congested and I was late.

By the time I arrived, the program had begun. I stopped by the buffet table, where a young waiter graciously offered to help me.

I rarely ate at programs, but opted for a small plate of tropical fruits: papaya and pineapple. As I sat down, various people eagerly introduced themselves. Then the Governor of Oregon began speaking.

When the event ended, I felt drained, as I often did at events, because people either talked at me or asked me to help their children get internships.

Afterward I walked to a notorious shopping district. As I wandered into a building that was set up like an outdoor market with rows of stalls and shops, I sensed I was being followed. I figured that aggressive dealers had spotted me, and were tracking me like hunters ready to pounce on their prey.

I took the escalator up to the third floor, where I tried on various *qipao* dresses. As I emerged from the changing room to study my reflection in the mirror, an overeager vendor urged me to make a purchase.

While I debated whether to buy it, I heard an American accent declare, "That dress suits you."

I wasn't surprised by the stranger's opinion since I was used to unsolicited comments. However, when I looked up, I was surprised to see a man who looked familiar.

"Do you remember me?" Aaron asked.

"Sort of," I replied while quickly ducking into the changing stall to change. "I suffer from a type of amnesia when I drink."

"Yeah, it's called a blackout."

"Mine are different," I said emerging from the fitting room.

"You left so unexpectedly. I went back to that club. The manager said you were married."

"I wasn't married at the time, but told people I was."

"Why?"

115

"A variety of reasons," I replied.

"So, you aren't married?"

"I am now," I said while handing the shop owner some *renminbi*.

"A woman like you shouldn't shop in markets like this," Aaron advised.

"Why?"

"The hesitation in your eyes … you could get eaten alive."

"Yet, here I am completely unscathed."

"Well, Mrs.—"

"Ms. Hayaak."

"After age thirty a woman's metabolism slows down. I can train you at the gym sometime."

"Thank you, but my weight is the least of my concerns. Goodbye."

I took off quickly so that I wouldn't be seen talking to Aaron. Otherwise, the driver, someone's maid, or my husband's office staff might see us and would invent gossip.

I hurried off to be alone. By the time I got home it was dark, as the sun set early in Shanghai, especially in the fall.

Curt was getting ready to attend a business dinner with Ben. As I entered our bedroom, he glanced over and asked, "How was your event?"

"Fine, but traffic was bad, so I was late and missed breakfast."

"Not surprised."

"Immediately upon arriving, a sales manager asked me to help him find a new job," I chattered mindlessly.

"Okay."

"So typical of events."

"Then why were you so eager to go?"

"I told you that I wanted to see Oregon's Governor. It was a quick program."

As if testing me, as opposed to actually caring, Curt asked, "So what did the Governor discuss?"

I took a deep breath and replied, "Did you know that Oregon has a statewide program whereby children learn Mandarin in elementary school?"

"Since when do you care about kids or public education?"

I reached up to fix my husband's tie and babbled nervously, "I just think it's so progressive."

"What did you do afterward?" Curt asked while leaving the bedroom and heading towards the front door.

"I went shopping," I replied, following my husband. I picked up Peter, who was climbing the curtains.

"Meet anyone special?" Curt asked as he opened the door to leave.

"Yes, an advertising director spontaneously struck up a conversation about Ron Paul," I responded.

"Lana, I'm not in the mood," Curt snapped as he exited.

CHAPTER 7
Curt Steiger

I sat at my desk reviewing documents, but couldn't focus. I was concerned about my wife's recent behavior. I always doubted Lana's emotional fidelity, but until recently, had never worried about physical disloyalty.

A few weeks ago, we went to a professional networking event in the *French Concession*. It was a casual affair. But Lana was suspiciously overdressed in her cocktail dress. Meanwhile everyone else wore shorts since it was hot.

The mixer was crowded, but we found seats. At first, Lana chatted with people. But within the hour she stood up and bolted for the door.

Initially I didn't analyze Lana's departure. I figured she went outside for fresh air, because cigarette smoke always bothered her. However, after an hour I became concerned. I texted her, but received no response.

When I got home, Peter was the only breathing creature in my apartment. Two hours later, Lana surfaced and claimed she went to a café to read her book.

Stressing about my wife's erratic behavior was interfering with my concentration. So I got up and went to my partner's office.

"Ben, I'm concerned about our drug tests. After months of trials, the results aren't good enough."

"I see," Ben responded. His eyes narrowed with a gleam of displeasure.

"The goal is to entice a large pharmaceutical company to purchase our program with an up-front payment of $60 million. Plus, milestone payments totaling $300 million and 15% royalties upon commercialization. Then by selling this program, our company's stock will increase."

"Yes, since you own 5% of this company's shares, you can sell your stock and make millions."

"I'll make $25 million," I said with measured enthusiasm.

"Sure, but *only* if there are positive results," Ben reminded me.

"Okay," I agreed.

"Figure out a way to fix it," Ben ordered.

CHAPTER 8
Curt Steiger

Per my daily routine, I was up before dawn and sat in our kitchen, where heat barely penetrated the cold, marble floors. Except for overhead fluorescent lights, the room was dim because the beveled glass windows prevented illumination. It didn't help that most days in Shanghai were overcast.

While eating cereal, I read the news on my iPad. Lana staggered into the kitchen with Peter hugging her heels. He loudly cried while demanding breakfast. My wife insisted on feeding him imported gourmet cat food.

Straight out of bed, without any makeup and her hair a mess, Lana looked very natural. She wore a long white cotton nightgown that was wrapped in a silk robe. She headed straight to the counter and opened a can of cat food. Peter nipped at her ankles.

"Ouch," Lana squealed as she spooned food into her cat's bowl.

"You're up unusually early," I remarked.

"I couldn't sleep because of *that* nightmare I always have."

"What nightmare?" I had no idea what she was talking about.

Lana babbled while absent-mindedly pouring too much creamer in her coffee. "I was at an airport in Moscow but had a four-hour layover, so I went into the city. I grabbed a taxi and asked the driver to take me to Kinko's, but he took me to some old library."

"There's a Kinko's in Moscow?" I asked with renewed interest. My wife's dreams rarely interested me.

Lana shook her head while accidentally placing dry cat food in the fridge. As she put creamer into the cupboard with the cat supplies she said, "I don't know since I've never been to Russia. But the taxi driver took me to an outdoor beer garden and insisted on buying me several rounds of beer."

I laughed. "Sounds like Munich, but *Oktoberfest* isn't for you."

Lana continued, "I panicked because I was running out of time. Suddenly, I had only thirty minutes left to catch my flight. I kept asking the taxi driver to take me back to the airport, but he refused. I was trapped and couldn't get back."

I nodded and suggested, "Your dream was about our recent trip to *Xi'an*. Remember how we almost missed our flight, because of the time *you* wasted with Peter?"

"Or maybe it means I feel disillusioned," she whispered.

I was angry because I suspected that she was taking a dig at our marriage.

I snapped, "Lana, the problem is whenever you don't want to do something you're never on time. Look at what happened during finals."

I didn't bother to mention her lax attitude regarding our wedding.

"Curt, I told you that story in confidence and now you're using it against me?"

"You need to be more prepared."

Lana was suddenly quiet, so I changed the subject and asked, "Have you chosen your Halloween costume?"

"But Peter, it's still only September,"

"My name is Curt. I know it's only September, but you love this time of year."

"I love autumn; however, I don't like holidays."

"Why?"

"They're so contrived. Every day should be a party," she suggested.

I laughed and said, "That's more like you."

"Who should I be for Halloween?"

"Rachel from *Blade Runner*."

"Your favorite movie," Lana acknowledged. "I suppose it was your dream to marry a woman who says practically nothing."

"Then I didn't hit that jackpot, did I?"

Lana playfully hit my shoulder and was more cheerful, which gave me *mild* satisfaction.

CHAPTER 9
Lana Hayaak

Curt was out of town visiting contract labs in *Suzhou*, a nearby town famous for its gardens and rivers. I sat on my white silk sofa in the living room talking to Colleen. Peter initially sat on my lap, but jumped down when he sensed tension in my voice.

"Natalia, calm down, why are you so upset?"

"Why did you give Cal my new name and contact info?"

"He's harmless, why care?"

"I thought you understood that I wanted to keep my new identity private," I said with frustration.

"Sure, but Cal stopped by our espresso shop and was so nice." Colleen and Margaret, friends from high school, were now business partners.

"Cal is not nice. If you saw the emails he sends, you'd understand." *Why didn't others pick up on the obvious?*

"Aw, he's in love," Colleen teased.

"This is not love. It's a perversion; besides, I'm married."

"Why are you making such a big deal?"

"Why give Cal my email, phone number, and home

address when I specifically asked you to keep my personal information private?" I obsessively repeated.

"Stop blaming me," Colleen asserted.

I heard movement at the front door. I jumped up, crept slightly closer to the door, and swore that I saw the doorknob turn. Instinctively, I backed away, darted into the kitchen, grabbed a knife, and started pressing the security button.

"Natalia, are you there?"

"Colleen, I have to go," I said and abruptly hung up.

Within minutes, two security guards and the manager entered my home with staged formality. After thoroughly inspecting my apartment, they explained that the CCTV cameras had recorded my drunk neighbor lurking in the hallway.

"How did he almost open my door?" I demanded.

"Well, ma'am, everyone in this apartment building has the same key."

"Lovely," I said sarcastically.

After thanking the staff, I changed into a long, white sundress with red trimmings. While dressing, I heard a knock at the door.

Security, again? I ran to the door, peeked through the peephole and was startled to see Ben Chang.

I liked my husband's partner because he was always kind. Unlike Curt's other friends, Ben was genuine, a good listener, and pleasant company.

FLASHBACK 2008

It was the end of the fall semester, and Curt invited me to his friend's birthday party at a Spanish tapa bar in the SoMa district of San Francisco. When I arrived, I saw Curt at the bar with his friends. He looked up to say 'hi,' but then focused his attention on a skinny brunette wearing a short, tight dress. I attempted to chat with some guests, but felt awkward. I stood alone for a while until Ben approached. He introduced himself as Curt's friend, bought me a drink, and asked, "What books have you read lately?"

I was surprised because I didn't expect deep conversation at this party. But I responded, "I'm reading a book about the American Civil War. It's kind of a passion."

"Why?"

"There's so much to learn from people who've lost —"

Suddenly Curt slapped his friend on the back and interjected, "Then you'll learn plenty from Ben."

Ben ignored the remark and asked, "Lana, what were you saying?"

"Victors rarely analyze their mistakes," I responded.

"That's your problem," Curt said to me.

"My problem?" I asked.

"You overanalyze everything."

I ignored Curt and said, "Ben, do you want to dance?"

As Ben and I headed to the dance floor, Curt shouted, "Lana, you have no sense of humor."

I replied, "Steiger, do you get tired of saying that to women?"

"Ben, what a surprise," I said as I opened the door. "Please come in."

"Thank you," Ben responded as he entered. "I just got back from visiting the labs in *Suzhou*."

"Cool," I said while pouring him a glass of water.

"Curt asked me to check on you."

"How thoughtful of him," I remarked dryly. "Ben, I'm meeting a friend for dinner. Can you join us?"

"Sure, I'd love to."

***

During the taxi ride, Ben asked, "Can you speak Chinese now that you've lived here for more than a year?"

"Not really. I'm tone deaf."

"I see."

"You have such a beautiful accent, Ben."

"Thank you, Lana, but how can you tell if you're tone

deaf?"

Changing the subject, I said, "We'll be dining at the same type of place where we first met."

"Lana, I'm impressed by your memory."

"Thank you. I have a knack for remembering all types of inconsequential details."

"I see."

We suddenly arrived at a location and jumped out too quickly. While standing on the corner, I realized I didn't know where to go. I began reviewing text messages from Eric.

"So typical of taxi drivers. They love to dump you off where it's convenient for *them*."

Ben patiently listened to my complaints.

"Can you read Mandarin?" I asked.

"Yes."

I handed Ben my cell, and he quickly read my texts. "Lana, the restaurant is across the street."

While crossing the street, Ben grabbed me as a motorcycle sped by.

"Ben, you saved me."

We climbed the staircase, but I slipped in my heels and fell.

"Lana, are you alright?" Ben said as he helped me up.

"I think I need new heels," I replied.

When we reached the second floor, I saw my handsome friend sitting in the corner. Eric was a very clean-cut, blonde with aristocratic features. He illuminated the dimly lit Spanish restaurant with his effervescent charisma.

I exclaimed, "Sorry, but we got a bit lost. Luckily, Ben helped me."

Eric smiled and said, "No worries. I just got here."

"This is my husband's partner, Ben," I responded.

The men shook hands, and Ben asked, "Are you a lawyer?"

Eric shook his head and replied, "I handle finance stuff;

however, I'm very concerned about corporate governance issues."

"Like what?" Ben asked.

"We've contracted with a company owned by a relative of the operations manager."

"Not uncommon," I remarked.

"This would never happen back home," Eric protested.

"You'd be surprised," I joked.

"Lana, you've changed," Eric declared.

"How?"

"Corruption used to infuriate you," Eric replied.

"The real world has jaded me," I confessed. "How is everything else?"

"Okay, but I'm sick of adults who giggle and carry stuffed animals," Eric responded.

"Seems harmless," I remarked.

"Sure, until they screw the boss," Eric exclaimed. "Then we all suffer."

I now turned to Ben and said, "I trust your office isn't like *that*."

Ben didn't say anything, because the waiter had returned to take our orders.

After we finished a leisurely dinner of tapas, paella, and sangria, Ben grabbed the check and insisted on paying. The three of us then strolled outside, where the nearby clubs were starting to generate energy. I could smell cigarette smoke in the air.

I hugged Eric goodbye and he hailed a taxi.

"Lana, I'll take you home," Ben promised.

"It's okay Ben. I'm a big girl; I can get home by myself."

"I insist. Curt would kill me if anything happened to you."

"Um, okay."

"Your friend Eric is very … interesting."

"What do you mean, Ben?"

"His comments—"

"Ah, well … Eric is very idealistic," I explained.

"He's gay, isn't he?" Ben said matter-of-factly.

"How did you know?" I asked with surprise.

"A variety of reasons. I guess it's not easy for someone like Eric to live in China."

Without thinking, I blurted, "Trust me, there are worse places he could be."

I immediately regretted my candor because Eric didn't want people to know he was gay. His supervisors were openly homophobic, which was the real source of his discontent. I realized that bringing Ben to dinner had inhibited a more honest discussion.

"I see," Ben responded with a grave look in his eye.

CHAPTER 10
Curt Steiger

A week after my trip to *Suzhou*, I hung out with Ben in *Xintiandi*. It was Happy Hour, and we drank scotch at an outdoor pub while tourists snapped shots of the historic area with their overpriced equipment.

"How's the purchase?" I asked.

"I gave *them* the number you suggested."

"Okay, so now we wait for their counter."

"Besides work, how are things?"

"I'm stressed about Lana."

"Why?" Ben asked.

"She's been acting weird."

"Lana was fine when I saw her last week."

"Yesterday, I ran into the MD of one of our competitors. His wife mentioned seeing Lana with some guy."

Ben shrugged. "Idle gossip."

I felt tense and said, "I've heard too many stories from other people."

"Do you mean Cindy? I don't think your ex-girlfriend is a reliable source."

"Good point," I agreed.

Ben narrowed his eyes. "I'm more concerned about Lana's friend Eric."

"You think she's involved with a gay guy?"

Impatiently Ben snapped, "No, I think Eric is a spook."

"Huh?"

"I think Eric is CIA."

"Why?"

"Eric's father is ex-military. He went to Georgetown and is fluent in Mandarin."

"So what? That's like every other person in Shanghai."

Ben was now vexed and asked, "Why is he friends with Lana?"

I shrugged. "They worked together and kept up the friendship."

"Gay men, especially Eric's type, don't hang out with women like Lana.

"They don't?"

"Real life isn't *Sex and the City*," Ben remarked dryly.

"How do you know so much about gay men?"

"I know a lot about many things."

"Okay."

"I fear Lana may be leaking sensitive data to Eric."

"Who is getting paranoid now?"

"This is serious. Focus because we're up against major issues."

"Okay, okay … I'm focused," I promised, but I was drowsy from too many drinks.

"The pre-clinical data is flawed, so let's speed up this deal."

"Are you saying we should alter the data?" I asked.

"I didn't say that *you* did."

"Ben, you sound like a lawyer."

"The data —"

I interrupted, "It'll be difficult to falsify once it's tested in humans."

"Figure it out quickly."

"Don't worry. I'll make sure it works."

"Good."

"Thing is, why should Lana get rich from this?"

Ben was annoyed, "Are we seriously talking about *her* again?"

"Yeah, if we divorce, she'll walk away with half of what I make from this deal, which would be $12.5 million."

"So divorce her," Ben suggested.

"It's not that simple. Lana can't touch any of the money I made before our marriage. However, she's entitled to half of everything I acquired after we married."

"We can't stall this deal while you divorce Lana to avoid paying her," Ben said impatiently. "Didn't you guys sign a prenup?"

"I made her sign an agreement whereby if she commits adultery, then she's not entitled to any community property."

"Is that even possible?" Ben asked skeptically.

"I hope so. I drafted the agreement myself."

"Look, this is getting so convoluted," Ben said looking at his watch. "Why don't we hire someone to follow her?"

"Like a private investigator?"

"More like a babysitter, so we can work out the kinks of our deal without interference."

"Okay."

"Good, now let's get dinner." Ben motioned to catch the waiter's attention.

***

A private investigator isn't necessary, Ben thought. *After all, secrets in Shanghai are not easy to hide.*

Ben's company kept a close eye on all of its associates and their spouses. What a surveillance camera couldn't catch, the maids, concierge, doorman, chauffeur, and staff surely would. The private investigator was a way to calm

Curt. That way, he could focus on his work.

From what Ben saw, Lana was very social and went out a lot, which caused the staff to gossip. However, if anyone would be the impetus for the dissolution of their marriage, it was Curt.

Lana had spent the summer in California, while her husband worked in Shanghai. One day, Ben walked past his partner's office. The door was slightly ajar. Curt was on the phone, shouting in a very authoritative voice, "I'm swamped and don't have time. From now on, if you want to call me, then politely text and say, please, Curt, please, please call me. Then, I'll make time for you."

Ben instinctively knew that Curt was shouting at a woman who was not his wife.

CHAPTER 12

Aaron was back at his office in *Guangzhou*, where his partner Troy ran a manufacturing facility. He entered the old warehouse, which was filled with fluorescent lighting. Boxes were stacked throughout the dusty room.

"How was Shanghai?" Troy asked. He was an elderly man with deep-seated wrinkles, scars, and white hair. Seated at a rusty desk, he studied intel on an old laptop.

"Great," Aaron replied, but he looked tired.

"You'll need to return, soon."

"Why?"

"We've got a new project."

"That's great, we need the business," Aaron admitted while taking a seat opposite of Troy. He grabbed a stack of papers, rifled through them, and said, "Bills are piling up."

Troy nodded and said, "Our new subject is the wife of a pharmaceutical executive."

"Okay."

"Born in Kuwait, Natalia Canaan was living in Kuala Lumpur when she was a teenager."

"Didn't you have special assignments there in the late nineties?"

"Yep, in that region. Natalia's father, Jason Canaan, was an Asian American vet. He was awarded the purple heart after surviving a Viet Cong prisoner of war camp."

Aaron nodded. "Admirable."

"Not exactly," Troy said sternly.

"What do you mean?" Aaron asked while setting the stack of bills aside.

"He was never a hero."

"Why do you say that?"

"Many of us figured that Jason sacrificed his men to get released by the Viet Cong. He was a shrewd guy and spoke many languages, including theirs."

"How do you know?" Aaron asked with mild skepticism.

"We never had any hard evidence. It was only circumstantial, but Canaan was always a self-serving bastard."

"If you say so," Aaron responded as he got up and walked over to a small table with a microwave and hot-water machine. He made himself some *oolong* tea.

"The government sent Canaan to Georgetown. He worked briefly as an architect, but then joined the DEA in the eighties. He and his wife worked undercover."

Aaron listened.

"But they were greedy. It happens to a lot of agents. They get sucked into the lavish expat lifestyle and aren't satisfied with a government salary."

"Sure," Aaron agreed while leaning back in his chair.

"Jason was on the take. He was doing the same stuff in Malaysia that he did in Vietnam."

"So what happened to him?"

"Jason and his wife were dragged out of their beds in the middle of the night."

"By the DEA?" Aaron asked.

"Nope, by the opposition. Probably for questioning."

Aaron nodded and asked, "How do you know?"

"Natalia was left at home. If the goal was to kill them, then they would have killed the entire family in their beds."

"Okay," Aaron said while sipping his tea.

"Things didn't go as planned which is typical. Accidents happen. People get killed."

"But the girl escaped?"

"Yeah, Natalia got away. The maid sent her to live with her grandparents or something. Someone was supposed to track her down but got sidetracked. Mistakes happen."

"Why didn't anyone go after her?"

Troy shrugged and said, "It became too much trouble. The FBI kept an eye on her. She was supposed to go into foster care, but there wasn't room and she got by on her own. Ultimately, Natalia was the perfect bait for attracting either (1) her parents; in case they had staged their disappearance, or (2) the group that killed Lara and Jason Canaan.

"Alright, thanks for the briefing," Aaron said while glancing at the overhead clock.

"Keep this job professional," Troy ordered.

"Don't I always?" Aaron asked.

Troy coughed. "Natalia Canaan is damaged goods."

"Why do you say that?"

"The apple doesn't fall far from the tree."

"No one is perfect," Aaron said while standing up and grabbing his gym bag.

"It's one thing to be flawed; it's another thing to be a two-faced traitor," Troy shouted as Aaron headed to the door.

"Why blame the kid for what her parents did?" Aaron asked.

"Just remember, abandoned kids are full of emotional baggage."

"You say that like you've got personal experience."

CHAPTER 13
Daniel Petersen

Through the narrow alleyways of the congested city, Daniel pedaled his bike as fast as he could to get to a new assignment.

Meanwhile, Curt and Ben sat in their Shanghai office on *Huai Huai Lu*, waiting for the arrival of a private investigator who had been recommended through contacts.

Neither Curt nor Ben wanted Daniel to know that they were concerned about the information Lana had regarding their impending pharmaceutical deal, or the possibility that she might report it.

"Okay, Daniel so here's the thing. My wife is a very jealous woman because she's insanely insecure," Curt explained while sitting imperiously behind his desk.

Daniel said nothing and stared at the picture of Lana on the desk, because she looked very familiar. Daniel was certain he had met her, but couldn't remember when or where. It was hard to believe this woman would be jealous over a guy like Steiger.

Curt continued talking, "You know how it is, Daniel. A guy like me can get any woman in China — anywhere and anytime. That's quite devastating to a woman like Lana, whose self-esteem is based entirely on her looks."

Daniel nodded and said, "Gotcha, my clientele is mostly female. My usual cases involve spying on husbands, lovers — well, you get the picture. Or, every now and again, some rich party girl gets knocked up and needs me to hunt down the father of her child."

"Uh, huh," muttered Curt, who was bored by these details. He was too self-centered to care about other peoples' problems.

Daniel was thrilled by the prospect of getting paid to stalk a woman. Frankly, he was tired of tailing old geezers. Looking closer at the photo, Daniel suddenly realized she was the woman he met on the plane six years ago.

"It's Really Ralph," he exclaimed, practically spilling his tea.

"What?" Curt asked. He and Ben looked very confused by Daniel's sudden outburst.

Ben responded, "Daniel, there's no one here named Ralph."

"Sorry, it's an expression," Daniel fibbed.

"Um, okay. Daniel, do you have any questions?"

"Sure, what exactly do you expect me to find? You're the one fending off the women, so if the wife is sitting at home, jealous, what's the problem?"

"Good question …" Curt paused. "I'm concerned that my wife will seek revenge in some way. You know how women are. Lana is smart and has access to a lot of confidential company trade secrets."

Daniel nodded.

"I need you to follow Lana and find out who she's meeting with and what she says."

"Sure, no problem," Daniel responded.

"Okay, well here's a list of links to Lana's social-networking sites, as well as a copy of a novel Lana completed a few years ago, but never published. It might give you insight regarding what she could wage against me. Also, here's her list of contacts. However, I'm sure there are people not on it. I've also included her daily schedule."

***

After Daniel departed, Ben turned to his partner and asked, "What do you think of our PI?"

"Seems like an odd guy," Curt remarked.

"Yeah, he's been in Shanghai for too long."

"Not surprised. Does Daniel know much about our company?"

"I don't think so," Ben said cautiously.

"Lately Lana's behavior has been more unusual."

"How so?"

"It's like she's up to something," Curt replied.

"Then it's good we hired Daniel."

"If we can't figure her out, how will a stranger?"

"Let's see what he discovers."

Curt didn't say anything and began checking his lab notes.

"How are the lab results?"

"Good," Curt lied.

CHAPTER 14
Lana Hayaak

I furiously swam laps in our rooftop pool. As water splashed, I inhaled the fumes of chlorine while observing the gray, yet moody sky.

I loved that the terrace was empty, because I could collect my thoughts in peace. I always tried to live in the present, but running into Aaron brought back certain memories.

FLASHBACK — 2009

Aaron and I were at a popular nightclub in Shanghai. While he spoke, I began to feel dizzy. I wanted to leave, but when I looked towards the nearest exit, I saw Cindy, Amy, and Gwen approaching. I froze because I was having an adverse reaction to the alcohol I drank.

Aaron grasped my arm and whispered into my ear, "Lana, are you okay?"

"I need to go to the ladies' room." I said to the group.

"Sure," chimed Cindy and Gwen.

I took off and was grateful to find the restroom empty. I wanted to jump out of the window, so I climbed up on to the sink. While looking through the glass, I heard the door swing open.

"Lana, why are you on the counter?" Amy demanded.

"Thank god you're here. I saw a rat run by," I quickly lied.

"Gross," she remarked while suspiciously scanning the area.

"I think it ran into that hole in the wall," I said pointing to a crack in the corner.

In truth, I had never seen a rodent in China, except for a dead mouse at a market.

"Ah, okay, it's gone, so let me help you down."

Amy gave me her hand. She was a very tall, confident woman and I appreciated her gentle caring nature.

Once down, she smiled and said, "That guy you're with is so hot."

I laughed and said, "He's not my type."

"Not your type? Are you blind? What's your type?"

"I like guys who live in their mom's basement and never leave the house. Aaron spends way too much time outdoors."

"Very funny."

Nervously I babbled, "There's this old Chinese saying: a smart woman sleeps with a stupid man."

"Why would anyone say that?" Amy demanded. I'd forgotten she had a Master's in East Asian Philosophy.

"I can't remember who said it. Was it Confucius or possibly Sun Tzu?"

"Or maybe it was you?"

"Maybe," I agreed sheepishly.

"You're so endearing, Lana."

"Thanks."

"You should visit my family home near Beijing."

"I would love that," I responded enthusiastically.

With a stroke of her hand, Amy pulled out my hair tie, and said, "Lana, you're so beautiful with your hair down. Why don't you ever wear it this way?"

I got this question a lot and didn't know what to say except, "It's more comfortable to wear it up."

"True, but I always see you watching women who wear their hair down."

"You're very observant," I remarked nervously. Suddenly, I wanted to return to Aaron and the gang because this conversation made me uncomfortable.

When Amy and I finally returned, Cindy was whispering into Aaron's ear, and Gwen was squeezing his muscles.

I stopped swimming and bobbed in the water for a few moments. I bounced toward the edge of the pool and clasped the cold, metal railing. As I slowly climbed up the ladder and emerged from the pool, I became overwhelmed with dizziness. I dismissed it as the reaction one has from low blood sugar and spending too much time in the water.

I shivered as a cool breeze blew through my hair and pierced the hollow of my chest. I felt unease sensing someone was watching.

I wrapped a towel around my wet body and carefully crept to the locker room to avoid slipping.

I opened my locker in the ladies' room and found a note which read:

Natalia Canaan, we need to talk about your parents. Meet me at Crimson Tide, Thursday evening at 9:30 p.m.

I stared at the note with disdain. Except for high school classmates, people rarely called me Natalia. I legally changed my name when I turned eighteen. Even Curt didn't know my birth name or family history.

Who left this note and how? Is it some kind of cruel joke?

I cautiously tiptoed out of the locker room and peeked around the corner. There was not a person in sight. I stood still, dripping wet, and felt similar feelings that I often experienced as a teenager. I was certain that I wasn't alone and an intruder was lurking in the shadows. *Or was I a paranoid?*

I dressed quickly, went up to the health club attendees, and asked if they had seen anyone leave the message for me. The reception clerks' faces remained stoic, but they shook their heads.

Someone must have seen the person who left this note, I thought as I returned to the changing room.

I contemplated calling security and asking them to look at the CCTV cameras, but it seemed like too much trouble. Also, there weren't *supposed* to be any cameras in the women's locker room.

CHAPTER 15

Daniel questioned Curt's story, because it didn't make sense. The tension in his voice and refusal to make eye contact, indicated that he was hiding something. Plus, the guy was an overall weirdo, with his meticulous record of Lana's schedule. *Talk about anal*, Daniel thought.

At the same time, Daniel was eager to uncover Lana's shenanigans, because her persnickety behavior in 2009 had left him … befuddled. He had now been tailing her for a few weeks. Some days, Daniel watched her socialize with friends. On one occasion, he saw her meet a tall, blonde man for coffee near her apartment.

Lana wore a flowing dress and strolled casually towards a coffee shop while her friend sat outside. While approaching she said, "Hey, Brian, is everything okay?"

"Not really, my girlfriend of eight years broke up with me."

Lana feigned surprise as she asked, "I thought you were getting married?"

"We were, but I lost my job, and then my girlfriend."

"Funny how that happens," Lana remarked dryly.

"I'm going home to Sweden. I've applied to hundreds of

companies, but am consistently rejected."

"The job situation is pretty dismal," Lana said empathetically.

"I'm suffering from depression, because last year I had it all. I was employed, with a nice apartment and a doting girlfriend. I also had a lot of attention from other women."

"You're a great guy. You'll find another girlfriend."

"European women are too strong for me."

Lana didn't say anything. She was tired of this complaint.

"Brian, for people with high expectations, failing to achieve something feels like heartbreak."

Brian nodded and said, "Yes, I think I've had a huge hole in my heart ever since I lost my job."

"That's normal," Lana continued. "You're suffering more from *disillusionment* than heartbreak. Time and a new passion will heal your wounds."

Daniel was bored by this conversation. It was clear there was nothing romantic between the two. Although Brian probably liked Lana, it was obvious that the feeling wasn't mutual. As far as Daniel was concerned, she'd never go for an unemployed guy.

CHAPTER 16

Ben, Lana, and Curt sat together at an outdoor restaurant in the *French Concession*. The three typically ate brunch together on Sundays at popular Shanghai venues catering to expats.

Lana sipped her orange juice as a young Chinese waiter stopped by and said, "Ma'am, please be careful of your bag. There are many thieves in Shanghai."

She sighed, smiled warmly at the server, and pulled her satchel closer. "Everyone in Shanghai is so charming."

"Lana, you're such a flirt," Curt complained while shoveling potatoes into his mouth.

"What are you talking about?" Lana asked innocently.

"You don't think I see you batting your eyes at strangers?" Curt asked.

"I'm just being friendly," Lana protested.

Ben was quiet while observing the banter that was routine between Curt and Lana.

"Do you know why young men are so friendly with you?"

"Because Lana is so attractive?" Ben suggested.

"No, it's because she looks rich. It's that simple. So

Lana, don't let it go to your head."

"You're one to talk," his wife responded.

"What's that supposed to mean?" Curt demanded, while looking up from his iPad.

"Nothing, but just remember — I like my men tender and sweet. You're over forty, so I could trade you in for a younger model."

"Ha, ha, not funny. You're too old for coquetry," Curt said snidely.

"I'm not old!"

"You're not *that* young," Curt teased.

"Projection," Lana hissed.

Attempting to change the subject, Ben intervened and asked, "Lana, did you watch *Mad Max*?"

"I can't stand romantic films," Lana insisted while rolling her eyes.

"*Mad Max* is not a romantic movie," Ben replied.

"It is for Lana," Curt joked.

"I don't understand," Ben said.

"I've always had a fondness for the genuinely macabre," Lana explained.

"Like what?" Ben asked with feigned interest.

"Real life. Can I tell you about a haunting legal case?" Lana asked. Her spirits brightened at the prospect of telling a story. Her cheeks flushed, and her eyes widened.

Curt groaned. "No one wants to talk about legal cases."

"I do," Ben replied.

"Thank you, Ben. Curt, do you remember the first criminal law case we ever read?"

"Do I look like a nerd?"

"As a matter of fact —"

"What was this case, Lana?" Ben asked.

"*The Queen vs. Dudley, Stephens.*" It's a 19th century case about four men who wound up on a dingy off the African coast. They had only a can of turnips, but no water. After a few days, they caught a turtle and ate it raw."

"Yuck," Curt complained as he tossed his toast aside.

"Turtle is a delicacy in China," Ben shared.

"The men had to drink their pee," Lana continued.

"Lana, could you stop it! I'm trying to eat breakfast. This discussion is not very ladylike."

Lana ignored Curt. "They were starving and couldn't capture rain in their coats. So after several days, they were desperate."

"Please hurry up!" Curt demanded while looking at his watch.

"The three older men killed and ate the sick 17-year-old cabin boy."

"Yep, perfectly legal, it's called the law of necessity," Curt asserted.

"The English courts didn't think so," Lana countered. "How did you perform so well in law school? Did you actually read any cases?"

"I'm very logical. I don't project my feelings into things," Curt retorted. "Anyway, *that* kid was going to die eventually."

"Then *they* should have waited," Lana insisted.

"What happened?" Ben asked.

"A few days later, a ship picked up the three survivors. The men had the flesh and blood of the cabin boy under their fingernails."

"It's necessary to get rid of dead weight," Curt remarked.

"*Then* when will you fire Conrad?" Lana asked.

"How did you hear about Conrad?" Ben interjected.

"C'mon Ben, where do you think?"

"Your girlfriends?" Ben asked.

Lana nodded. "Gretchen and Shelley told me all about Conrad and his teenage girlfriend."

"Your friends should mind their own business," Curt suggested.

"How? Conrad is so indiscreet," Lana responded.

"So what?"

"Liability issues for your company," she asserted.

"Nah, not really, it's a private matter," Curt said smugly.

Ben agreed, "Curt's right. Conrad is a valuable chemist."

Lana exclaimed, "Conrad kicked his wife, Kitty, out of their apartment and his lover moved in."

"Quite unfortunate," Ben said.

Lana continued, "When Kitty attempted to re-enter, she assaulted the girlfriend, so Conrad called the police on his wife."

"None of your business!" Curt repeated.

"Except … we're in China," Lana countered. "Your company had to put up his work permit, which was a long and expensive process. The Chinese government could fine you or worse."

"Lana has a point," Ben admitted. "Where is Conrad's wife?"

"Gretchen's place. She's broke because Conrad won't give her any money," Lana replied.

"Conrad thinks he's *in love* and has never felt this way before," Curt rationalized.

Eric had popped up earlier and surreptitiously slid into a chair next to Lana. Familiar with the story, he said wryly, "Nah, Conrad isn't in love. He's just another old geezer in Shanghai, fucking a teenager. It's disgusting."

CHAPTER 17
Lana Hayaak

Rain showers drenched the city, while thunder erupted in the distance. Lightning pierced the dark sky belying the fact that it was only mid-afternoon.

I love October because there are generally plenty of horror films on TV, even in Shanghai with our limited cable selection. However, the only thing on today was a lewd comedy called *Deuce Bigalow: Male Gigolo*.

I heard Rob Schneider's character exclaim, "How did you get that job? I'm going to kill my guidance counselor," as I cuddled Peter and reflected on a dream:

I was trapped in a burning building in Eastern Europe. I ran through the hall towards a closed window, but couldn't get it open. When I looked out the window, I saw my parents in the streets. They looked up but didn't see me.

Peter nipped my leg, which disrupted my thoughts. I stood up, walked to the kitchen and fed my cat his dinner.

I dressed impatiently because I had a busy evening planned. First, I had to stop by the Expat Women's Club to visit friends. Then I was supposed to meet the person who had left the cryptic note in my locker.

CHAPTER 18
Daniel Petersen

I hid in the shadows, impatiently waiting for Lana to appear. It was 6:30 p.m. when she finally sauntered out of her apartment. Evidently, this lady of leisure was not in any hurry.

According to her calendar, she was supposed to meet friends at the Expat Women's Club. I was familiar with this group.

Lana stood on the marble steps in front of her apartment while waiting for her chauffeur. She wasn't dressed for a casual event, as she was wearing a white suit. It was like her uniform.

I hoped on my bike and followed her car. The driver delivered Lana to a bar on a cobblestone street in the *French Concession*. Once at her destination, she chatted with wives about typical expat complaints: maids, poor service, and shopping.

Meanwhile, I lingered at a table not far from Lana, but kept my back turned away from her. It was the perfect spot to listen in on her conversation.

"Sara, how's teaching?" Lana asked a middle-aged

woman who wore glasses and a short, curly hairstyle.

"It's great, but I feel my students need to understand religion if they're going to understand the United States."

"I see," Lana said. She paused for a moment, took a sip of orange juice and asked, "Do you think that's a good idea?"

Sara nodded and replied, "Yes, religion is the foundation of Western culture."

Lana struggled to be diplomatic and said, "Does the Chinese government allow religious studies in schools?"

"They don't, and it's wrong," exclaimed Sara, who appeared quite passionate about this issue.

I was bored.

Luckily, Sara changed the subject and asked, "Lana, are you alright? It seems like something is bothering you."

"I'm very well, thank you for asking," Lana responded.

"Please tell me what's wrong," Sara pleaded.

"I don't understand why strangers constantly barge up to me and ask if I'm Chinese," Lana declared.

Sara responded, "The only thing Asian about you are your eyes — only slightly — and your wrists.

At that moment Karen, a Canadian woman, spun around and blurted, "They're trying to find out if you're up for NSA."

"I beg your pardon," Lana responded with surprise.

"No strings attached sex," Karen clarified.

"And here I just thought they wanted to know my ethnicity," Lana said.

"Yes, because —" Karen tried to continue.

But Lana cut her off to say, "So if I'm Chinese —"

"Chinese women are conservative and want commitment," Karen asserted with conviction.

"How do you know all of this?" Sara interjected.

"I read it on a local blog: *Shanghai Genius*," Karen explained.

"Well if you read it on *Shanghai Genius* then it must be

true," Lana said playfully.

Sara piped in, "You're smearing American women."

Karen shrugged and said, "I'm not the judgmental one."

"What's that supposed to mean," Sara demanded.

"You're the one waving the Bible around like it's the U.S. Constitution. Frankly, the latter would be more useful to your students," Karen retorted.

"Well morals still matter — at least to me," Sara said firmly.

"What a woman does where, when, and with whom, is her business," Karen argued.

"Yes, but God is always watching," Sara finished.

Karen now turned to Lana and said, "There was a time in Canada when our news wasn't the rubbish you get in the U.S."

Lana nodded and said, "But now —"

Karen continued, "It's the same. Can you imagine how hard it was for me, as a young mother, trying to explain why your President Clinton got a —"

"He was never my president," Sara declared.

While Lana and her friends bantered I felt a heavy-set woman brush up against me. I looked up and realized it was Gloria Rivers. "Daniel, how are you?" she purred.

Gloria beamed from ear to ear while her eyes locked with mine. I felt queasy. This middle aged woman was a former client. Initially she hired me to spy on her husband, but as time progressed it was apparent that she wanted more. I didn't find Gloria particularly attractive, since she was overweight, overbearing, and wore the same fragrance as my granny.

"Mrs. Rivers, what a surprise to run into you," I responded in my debonair manner.

"Not really, you know that I come here regularly," she said with a sly grin.

"Uh, huh," I stammered.

"Daniel, are you stalking me?"

"Ha, ha Mrs. Rivers. You caught me."

"Daniel, call me Gloria," she ordered as she not-so-subtly inched closer.

I could feel the abundant weight of her body pressing up against mine. I scanned the room wondering if anyone was watching.

Gloria fondled my shoulder and said, "C'mon Daniel, one drink." I caught some guys at the pool table looking over. Some snickered, while one gave me a thumbs-up sign.

From the corner of my eye, I realized Lana was escaping. My adrenaline surged. I turned to Gloria and said, "I'll have to take a rain check. I just remembered that I forgot to put money in the parking meter."

"What meter, Daniel? There are no parking meters in Shanghai," she shouted while I bolted for the door.

As I dashed to the curb, I frantically looked around but didn't see Lana. Frustrated, I walked around in circles and finally found her driver. I pressed him about Lana's whereabouts, but he shrugged and buried his head in a newspaper. This was the second time Lana had pulled a disappearing act. I scoured the streets looking for her, but had no luck.

There were unexplainable gaps in Lana's day. *Occam's razor*: the simplest explanation is generally correct. I was disappointed because I thought my Batman was better than other women. Lana was so innocent when we met, but evidently I was wrong. Clearly, she was the same as any other desperate housewife and was having an affair.

I got a text from Curt. He was anxious and suggested meeting soon. I groaned because I hadn't found much.

CHAPTER 19
Lana Hayaak

When the rain finally stopped, I practically flew out of the Women's Club event and headed to the *Bund*. As I entered the moody, dimly-lit nightclub, I surveyed the room looking for the person who might have sent the note. Curious eyes glanced in my direction, but no one approached.

I headed to the bar, where I refused the free Ladies' Night drinks because they were a mixture of low-quality booze and syrup. I ordered a club soda and glanced at my phone.

Within minutes, a confident man in his early twenties slid up beside me and gave me a cunning look. Gently, he reached for a cocktail napkin, pulled out a designer pen, and scribbled something on it.

My curiosity piqued. I wondered if this was my mystery messenger.

He folded the napkin, seized my hand, and placed the message in it. He then took off to join a pack of men wearing suits. The group huddled on the open-air deck with a panoramic view of the city.

I unfolded the note which read: *Sex? 3,000 RMB?*

3,000 RMB was approximately $500. Was this young man selling his services, like the character in the Rob Schneider film I watched earlier?

I surmised that this brazen person had nothing to do with the message I received in the women's locker room.

I observed a flock of stunning women enter the club. They looked like fashion models and strolled on to the dance floor. So I joined.

While dancing, a middle-aged man slithered up, didn't dance, but blurted, "Did you come here alone?"

I ignored him because his question was impertinent. The guy then leaned into my ear and whispered, "You know that when you come here and dance with these women, people will think you're one of them."

"A model?" I asked.

"They're not models. They're prostitutes."

I flashed my ring and said, "I'm married. Please leave me alone."

"Where is your husband?" the creep demanded.

"Not that it's your business, but he's on a conference call with Switzerland."

"I'm very sorry, Ma'am. I didn't know you were married to someone working here."

"Why does that matter? Whether I'm married to anyone is neither here nor there."

I stormed off the dance floor to escape the wormy guy. I was heading for the exit when a German bachelor party entered. A young blonde approached and asked me to dance.

"Where are you from," he asked.

"San Francisco," I replied.

"I love San Francisco,"

"Are you from Munich?"

"How did you know?"

"Your accent," I responded.

"Your accent isn't American."

"I hear that a lot. Are you a student?"

"Yes, I am studying for my PhD in Finance, because everyone in Germany wants the title of 'doctor.'"

I laughed.

"What do you think of that woman dancing on the bar table?"

"She's very sexy."

"Yes, but she is a man."

"I can't believe that!" I exclaimed.

"Believe it. Do you know why it's better to be a gay man than a gay woman?"

"Why?" I asked too quickly.

"Because life is simple for men, we know what we want."

"I see."

The grad student continued, "Women are all about emotions. They're so complicated."

And with that, I took off.

CHAPTER 20
Lana Hayaak

The next day, I was at home getting ready for another event. I sat at my vanity applying makeup, while Peter slinked across my cosmetics.

Last night was an ordeal. It was like someone's idea of a sick joke. I vowed to ignore any future, enigmatic notes that I might receive.

Peter paused like a statue. His eyes glimmered as he stalked his prey. With the focus of a predator, Peter wiggled his derrière and pounced upon my hair band, which he batted aggressively. I attempted to cuddle him, but he squirmed, bounced on the bed, and sauntered away.

I continued to get ready while thinking about my mother.

FLASHBACK 1988

I was five years old, and she was tucking me into bed.
"Natalia, what do you want to be when you grow up?"
"A ballerina."
"Do you know what is even better than being a ballerina?
"What?"

My memory suddenly shifted.

FLASHBACK 2009

Sitting in a dark room.
"Ms. Hayaak, you've gotten very far in this process."
I nodded as it had been a year-long endeavor.
"To work for us, you'll need to …"

I heard an abrupt crash. Peter had leapt back onto my vanity, knocked over a glass, and jolted me out of my daydream. Realizing I was late, I grabbed my purse and dashed out of the apartment.

CHAPTER 21
Daniel Petersen

From a safe distance, I watched Lana. Today, she was at an event where she talked with various Europeans.

"What's your favorite city in Europe?" Lana asked a tall man with curly dark hair.

"Paris, my hometown," Pierre responded. "What's yours?"

"Dresden," Lana replied unequivocally.

"Why Germany?"

"Many reasons."

"I don't like Germans," Pierre complained.

Lana said diplomatically, "Rivalry between bordering nations is typical. Except for Canada —"

"History in America is so bad. Don't you know about World War 2?"

Lana was tired of Europeans ridiculing Americans, particularly their knowledge of history. As far as she was concerned, arrogance is synonymous with ignorance.

"On the contrary, that's all anyone seems to know. Can you tell me why World War 2 started?"

"Yeah, it was because of this guy named Hitler. Ever

heard of him?"

"He was the effect of World War 1, not the cause of —"

"Why do you even care?"

"Why bomb innocent civilians when Germany was almost defeated?"

Pierre took a swig of whiskey and declared, "Justice!"

"Is there such a thing?" Lana challenged.

"C'mon, don't be so passive." Pierre demanded.

Sitting, quietly by the bar, Paul nursed his beer while surreptitiously listening to Lana and Pierre. He then stridently marched up to the two and barked, "Lana, you need to leave."

"Excuse me?"

"We've received complaints about you."

"What?"

"You're creating a scene, *Mrs. Steiger.*"

"You're the one raising *his* voice."

"Your politics is alienating customers, so get out of here!"

"I'm leaving and don't worry, I won't return."

Lana looked quite haughty, while Paul burst into uncontrollable laughter.

"Ha, ha, Lana you should see yourself. Man, you looked pissed. I really got you."

Lana glared at the hysterical man as he wrapped his arms around himself tightly.

Finally, she said, "You're quite impressed with yourself, aren't you?"

Paul smirked. "You take yourself so seriously. No one cares what you think!"

Lana refused to respond as she threw a tip on the counter, turned around, and stormed out of the event. Before departing, a waiter dashed up and gave her a note. She paused to read it carefully.

I struggled to decipher her expression but could discern nothing. I snuck over to the waiter and asked if he knew who sent the message. But the guy was clueless. I paused and couldn't help thinking that it must be her lover.

From the corner of my eye, I spotted Lana grab a taxi, so I quickly followed her to the *French Concession*.

CHAPTER 22

The sky was black, but lit by a faint flurry of stars. The air was crisp and chilly, but smelled of jasmine. At *Xintiandi*, Lana met her friend Shelley. The two sat at an outdoor bar & grill. Soon they were joined by another couple: Matt, a good-looking marketing director from Boston and Kim, a voluptuous blonde from Vancouver.

"Did you guys see the debates?" Shelley asked.

Matt responded, "Yes, I'm rooting for —"

A stranger suddenly appeared and asked, "Hey, are you guys American?"

"I'm Canadian," Kim replied.

"I'm British," Shelley answered.

"Lana and I are American," Matt said.

"Nice to meet you. My name is Tomas Diaz."

"Where are you from?" Lana asked.

"Rio de Janeiro," Tomas responded while taking a seat next to Lana. "I'm a journalist."

"What are you writing about?" Lana inquired.

"Relations between China and Russia," Tomas replied.

Lana nodded and said, "That makes sense. Russia is now China's largest supplier of crude oil."

"Yes, since April, almost 930,000 barrels per day were sent to China."

"The conflict in Ukraine has brought China closer to Russia," Lana continued.

"Hey, you really *get* this," Tomas noted while sliding closer to Lana.

Matt, Shelley, and Kim listened politely, but looked bored.

Tomas was about to whisper something in Lana's ear when a booming voice shouted, "Hey, man why don't you get a little closer?"

Matt, Shelley, and Kim were now fully alert. They looked up and were startled to see a tall, athletic man.

"What's it to you?" Tomas demanded.

"Look pal I don't own her, but have some respect," Aaron responded.

"Respect?"

"Yeah, give the woman some space."

"Do you want to take this outside?" Tomas challenged.

"We are outside," Aaron replied nonchalantly.

Shelley burst into giggles, as the two men scowled at one another.

Lana turned to the slender Brazilian and implored, "Please don't worry about him."

"Who the hell does he think he is?" Tomas asked while almost shaking.

"This guy isn't worth your time," Matt advised.

Kim leaned in towards Shelley and whispered loudly enough for everyone to hear, "What is it with Americans?"

Shelley laughed and remarked, "Yeah, everything is always about force."

Tomas looked over at the women and asserted, "I'm not American. I'm from Brazil."

Kim nodded and said, "We weren't talking about you."

Shelley looked at Aaron and teased, "Yeah, we were referring to *Rambo*."

Everyone was distracted by the tension between Tomas and Aaron. Thus no one noticed that a stranger had surreptitiously slipped a message into Lana's purse.

Aaron looked at Shelly and joked, "You didn't have a problem with Americans the other night."

Shelley blushed.

Meanwhile, Lana got up and attempted to sneak away but Aaron clasped her elbow.

"Are you out of your mind? Let go of me!" she demanded.

Shelley shrugged and turned to chat with Tomas, who appeared more relaxed having downed a glass of wine shared by Matt and Kim.

"We need to talk," Aaron insisted.

"I don't need to do anything," Lana declared.

She grabbed her purse, waved a quick goodbye to her friends and headed towards the street. She anxiously ran towards a row of taxis.

Aaron followed and asked, "So what was Kuwait like?"

Lana stopped for a second because she was surprised by the question. However, she quickly regained her composure and retorted, "How would I know? Hot? We fought a war over it, or didn't you watch the news in the nineties?"

"Ha, ha … nice try, so how's the weather in Malaysia?"

"What do I look like, a weather app?"

Lana attempted to slide into the taxi when Aaron said, "Natalia Canaan, we *need* to talk."

Startled by the mention of her name, she whispered, "So you're the sender of the notes?"

"Notes? What are you talking about?"

"The note I found in my locker," Lana explained.

"Do I look like a guy who would leave a note in your locker?"

"Um, uh" Lana stammered.

"No! Now get in the car. We need to talk."

CHAPTER 23
Daniel Petersen

I sat on a park bench in the *Jing'an District*, reading Lana's unfinished novel. Nearby, groups of senior citizens practiced *Tai Chi* while other people played classical Chinese music on handmade instruments.

Despite the sounds of traffic on *Huai Huai Lu* and parents playing with their infants, I was engrossed in the manuscript Steiger had given me.

I was surprised, because it wasn't what I expected. Curt had suggested it was a book about Japanese prisoner of war camps. But apparently, Lana's husband had never read it, because it was more like a diary. It included absurdly flowery entries like — "*You see officer … I suppose it all began on a warm summer's day, but to go back in time would surely exhaust the reader…*"

I didn't find the diary particularly helpful. I figured that this journal was not intended to be private. *After all, why would Lana leave it out for anyone to read?* Batman was a suspiciously secretive person, and I figured that these entries were made up to support an illusion of someone she pretended to be.

I looked at my watch and realized that I needed to go home to change because I was meeting with Curt and Ben. I had expected to engage with them privately. But instead, they invited me to join their office party at a luxury hotel by the riverside.

When I arrived at the rooftop reception, the venue was fairly empty. I encountered the men and asked, "Aren't you concerned that I'll blow my cover with Lana?"

"Knowing Lana, she won't remember you," Ben assured me.

"But then she'll recognize me," I protested.

"At this point, it doesn't matter," Ben responded.

I realized that I'd be replaced if I didn't produce any useful information.

"Have you actually learned anything?" Curt asked.

"A few things," I replied.

"Such as?" pressed Ben.

"Lana wrote about how much she cares about some guy named Peter."

Curt impatiently snapped, "Yeah, and a cat named Larry?"

"I have more," I promised and handed Curt a flash drive.

"It'll have to wait, because Curt and I need to speak with someone," Ben said.

I ordered a G&T from the rooftop bar and took a lounge seat in the open-air patio while surveying the room. Things were quiet. Lana hadn't yet arrived.

I noticed Lana's friend Eric and Curt's IT guy, Kamlesh Khan, so I walked over to join them. Kamlesh was a sanguine man, of South Asian descent, from Nova Scotia. He was in his late-20s and had a friendly disposition.

"How do you guys like living in China?" I asked after quick introductions.

"It's great. We were just discussing the differences between Beijing and Shanghai," Eric replied.

I asked, "Which city do you prefer?"

"Shanghai since I have a girlfriend here," Kamlesh answered.

"I prefer Beijing because folks are more serious," Eric opined.

I nodded.

"People in Beijing are less demonstrative," Eric continued.

"Yeah, compared to other places, where people shove their love life in your face," I said.

"Like on Facebook," Kamlesh agreed.

"I have a theory: when a couple is super affectionate in public, it means they're about to break up," Eric proposed.

"Yeah, we should start a data mining company based on that," Kamlesh suggested. "Collect data on couples that post the most obnoxious PDA photos. Then sell that information to divorce lawyers."

I jumped in and said, "Hey, that's a great idea. So what's the story with Steiger and his wife?"

"What do you mean?" Eric asked.

"Are they demonstrative in public?" I clarified.

"Not that I've ever seen. In general, Lana is pretty standoffish, and Curt is obsessed with his work," Kamlesh responded.

"What kind of a name is Hayaak anyway?" I asked.

"It's Lebanese, isn't it?" Eric suggested.

"Lana looks like a Tartar from the Crimea," I opined.

"Actually, she looks mixed, like the girls from Turkmenistan, Uzbekistan, or Xinjiang," Kamlesh pointed out.

It was now 10 p.m. As the party intensified, Lana entered. She glanced around, ordered a drink at the bar, and casually strolled out on to the terrace. Lana spent a minute with Ben and Curt before working the room. She took the time to greet almost everyone.

As Lana left the exterior part of the deck, I saw her look

in my direction. She approached our group and sat down next to Eric. Before Kamlesh or Eric could say anything, Lana turned to me and said, "Hello."

"You look very familiar," I said.

"Do I? I don't think we've met," she responded extending her hand. "How are you? My name is Lana."

"Hi, my name is Daniel, are you sure you don't recognize me? I swear I've seen you stalking me all over town."

Lana studied me without any expression. She took a sip of wine, turned to Kamlesh and Eric and said, "Hey, guys, what's up!?"

"Not much, Lana. When will you head back to California?" Eric asked.

Lana smiled. "Not until Christmas, but we'll probably head to Chicago to see Curt's Dad."

Kamlesh continued, "I would kill to live in California, especially Silicon Valley."

Lana responded, "Yes, plenty of blue skies."

Eric remarked dryly, "Yeah, but in Lana's world the skies are always gray."

Batman ignored Eric and said, "Kamlesh, I'm sure Curt will bring you back with us."

Lana deliberately ignored me. I couldn't believe she didn't recognize me. Apparently, she hadn't seen me lurking in the shadows and didn't remember me from 2009. This sort of made sense, since I had gained fifty pounds and grown a beard.

Years ago, Lana had teased, "Daniel, you have the skin of an angel. It's even lovelier than the complexion of a Korean pop singer." She then analyzed my palms, batted her eyes flirtatiously and whispered seductively, "Mr. Petersen, you have the hands of a gentleman. I don't think you've ever even changed the oil of a car." It was then that I knew Batman wanted me. I was used to reeling women in with my witty humor. Lana was the first attractive woman who "negged" me. And I was convinced that even now, her evasive behavior was her way of playing hard to get. Or, maybe Batman was fighting her feelings because she was married to a lunatic.

Lana got up to leave, but Eric exclaimed "Don't leave. We were just talking about social media."

Smiling, she asked, "Is that so?"

"Yeah," Kamlesh chimed in, "we were talking about starting our own data mining company."

"Is my husband's company that boring? Don't worry; your secret is safe with me."

She gazed across the room and observed Curt, who was very drunk and overly flirtatious with his secretary, a slim attractive local. I studied Lana's face, but she was stoic.

Kamlesh was eager to distract her, so he said, "I was kidding. We were just saying it's obnoxious the way people broadcast their relationships online."

"I've noticed," Lana responded.

Is she serious? I wondered. Lana didn't seem to notice or care about anything. There was something vacant about her.

"According to an article, there's an inverse relationship between online romantic posts and self-esteem," Lana shared.

Kamlesh nodded and said, "Yep, same for the folks who post selfies."

Ben now walked over and sat down next to Lana.

"And if someone posts pictures of their children, I'll presume that they aren't drug dealers," she continued.

Ben looked at Lana intently and said, "It sounds like you know a lot about drug dealers."

"Not at all," the pharmaceutical executive's wife insisted. Apparently, she saw no relationship between FDA-approved drugs and narcotics.

Ben clasped Lana's hands tenderly and said, "I'm always impressed by your interest in even the most esoteric of things."

"Thank you, Ben. I'm sure you agree that we hide what we value most."

"Indeed, we do," he agreed.

"How's the project?" she asked, suddenly changing the subject.

"Very good. I can't say much, but we've made great progress."

"That's wonderful," Lana exclaimed.

"Soon, your husband can slow down and you can start a family."

"God, I hope not."

Ben looked disturbed. "You don't want children?"

"Definitely not."

"Lana I'm surprised to learn this."

"Children are too noisy and time-consuming," she complained.

"I see," Ben responded. "So, what have you been doing lately?"

"Trying to decide what my tombstone should say."

Eric interjected, "Are you serious?"

"Yes," Lana replied.

Kamlesh asked, "What have you chosen?"

"I want my grave to say, 'It's a blessing and a curse to know what people are thinking. It's like being Sookie Stackhouse in *True Blood*.'"

I listened carefully and couldn't help thinking that Lana Hayaak was even more peculiar than I had ever imagined.

***

As Lana was chatting with Kamlesh and Eric, Ben and I went over to speak with Curt. I quickly explained my findings to both men.

Curt then marched up to his wife, interrupted her and said, "Please come with me."

She rose and asked, "Sure, where are we going?"

Curt didn't answer, but she followed him to a private

room. Ben and I joined.

"Why are they here?" Lana demanded. Ben and I took seats by the wall.

"A variety of reasons," Curt said brusquely. He figured he might need witnesses in the future. Lana turned to leave.

"Not so fast," Curt snapped, while Ben locked the door.

Lana looked anxious now that she was trapped.

Curt began removing photographs from an envelope and laid them out on the table. His tone was serious as he stated, "You've got some explaining to do, please sit down."

"What are you talking about?"

Curt pointed to photos of his wife. The first one included Aaron at the market.

"How did you get that?" Lana asked with surprise.

"We have our ways," Curt answered smugly.

I said nothing because I had not shot those pictures. *It must have been the driver*, I thought.

"It was an accident that I ran into Aaron," Lana said defensively.

"Since when do you believe in coincidences?"

She crossed her arms. "He came up to me out of the blue."

"Isn't he the same man you met in 2009?" Curt demanded.

"Who I consorted with before we married is none of your business," she hissed.

"Maybe, but you've continued meeting."

"We haven't."

"Then what were you doing at *Crimson Tide* last Thursday?" Curt produced pictures of his wife dancing with the German student at a bachelor party.

"Long story," she replied.

Curt next removed pictures of Lana sitting next to the Brazilian journalist. Then he pulled out photos of her with Aaron as they were leaving the grill together.

"So what's going on?" Curt asked.

"I can explain. It's not what it looks like," Lana exclaimed.

Ben and I watched in silence.

"You left with this guy?" Curt demanded.

"Yes, but it was only to talk during the taxi ride. Aaron dropped me off at *People's Square*, and I took the subway home."

"Talk? Do you expect me to believe that?"

"Yes, because it's the truth. *Let me explain*," Lana continued.

I fought to suppress laughter. At the rate Lana was going, her tombstone would read: Let me explain.

As if Lana read my mind, she suddenly regained her poise and asserted, "On second thought, I don't have to explain *anything*. I never pry into your life, but here you are intruding into mine and humiliating me in front of these two."

No one said anything for a few seconds, but then Lana ordered, "Open the door, right now!"

"Okay, I'm sorry," Curt apologized. "I've been so stressed with work. You were about to explain something?"

Lana looked as if she were contemplating whether to storm out of the room or talk. Finally, she said, "When I was fifteen, we were living in Kuala Lumpur. One day my parents vanished. Recently, I started receiving cryptic notes promising information regarding their whereabouts. I went to the club because of the first note. When I received the second, I ignored it, but Aaron initiated contact. He insisted on sharing a cab so that he could share info."

"You said your parents died in a car accident when you were nineteen," Curt reminded his wife.

"I wanted to keep things simple."

"There's nothing simple about you. I don't even know who you are."

"Curt, we barely dated and you've never shown any

interest in my background."

"I'm listening now."

"Too little, too late," Lana declared.

"So what did you learn about your parents?" Curt asked with a genuine degree of interest.

"Aaron insists I meet him again to explain what happened to Mom and Dad. He suggested that my parents are alive and in Beijing."

"And you believe him?" Curt asked. "The guy sounds like pure sleaze."

Ben finally interjected, "Why would your missing parents be in Beijing?"

"Consulting for the Chinese government," Lana replied. There was hope in her eyes.

"In your dreams," Curt countered callously.

Lana looked hurt.

"I think this guy is a con artist seeking to extract money," Ben opined.

"But what if he's right? What if my parents are still alive?"

"Then why haven't they contacted you?" Ben asked.

CHAPTER 24

The office party was over, and everyone had left, including Lana and Daniel. Curt and Ben talked privately on the balcony of the hotel.

"Lana's story is interesting," Ben said diplomatically.

Nursing a glass of whiskey, Curt thought for a moment and then said, "I think she believes this bullshit."

"Uh, huh," Ben responded.

"My little Lana is more naive than I ever imagined."

"Do you actually think that's the case?" Ben asked.

"Yes, Lana is a damaged creature. She'll believe anything because it's what she wants to hear."

"Exactly, which is why we have to keep her away from this con-artist," Ben insisted.

"Yeah, of course," Curt agreed.

"How much does Lana know about our company's work?"

"Hard to say."

"Daniel noted that she never discussed anything related to the business."

Changing the subject, Curt asked, "How are negotiations?"

175

"The deal with *this* buyer is fine," Ben replied.

"Lana is so incredibly secretive," Curt complained.

Ben nodded and said, "Even if your wife knew anything, I don't think she would share company trade secrets."

"Why do you say that?"

"When I was at dinner with Lana, there was an opportunity for her to share things with Eric, but she kept quiet."

"True, and technically she benefits from any money I make."

"Exactly Curt, why would she want to screw things up?"

"Things don't add up with Lana."

"What do you mean?"

"Do you believe the story about her parents?" Curt asked.

"Not really," Ben admitted.

"After graduation, Lana went MIA. When I probed her, she gave me a roundabout explanation regarding a marketing job."

Ben shrugged. "Yeah, I vaguely recall that discussion at one of your parties."

"Yep, we pinned Lana down, and she said she worked at offices in Boston and D.C."

Ben nodded.

"Thing is, I had friends working in those cities," Curt continued. "No one I knew ever saw Lana."

"Maybe she was busy and didn't go out much," Ben suggested.

"When I asked Lana where she worked, she couldn't answer."

"What's your point?" Ben demanded.

"When has Lana ever been honest about anything?"

"Your wife is as ambiguous in appearance as she is in character."

CHAPTER 25
Daniel Petersen

After the party, Lana didn't go home with the company driver. Instead, she hurried to the subway station and ran down the stairs.

I followed her and watched while she patiently waited for a nervous local who was taking an inordinate amount of time at the ticket machine. The man couldn't find his change, because he was blind. Distressed, he started to leave as people were loudly complaining. Lana reached into the machine to retrieve his coins. She then chased after the blind man and gave him his money.

Having lost her place in line, I took the opportunity to say, "Hey, Lana, I'm really sorry about what happened."

"Why?" she demanded while refusing to look at me.

"It's a coincidence that your husband hired me to follow you."

She relaxed and said, "It's okay."

I seized the chance to ask, "Are you in love with that guy, Aaron?"

Her mood changed abruptly, and she responded, "Why do you think that?"

"It's obvious through your body language and facial expressions."

"You need a new job because you're not very perceptive," Lana retorted.

"Hey, I correctly predicted the outcome of *that* couple."

"What are you talking about?"

"2009 ..."

For a split second Lana looked wistful as she whispered, "That was a long time ago." But she quickly regained her poise and purchased a subway ticket from the machine.

"I'm very observant," I asserted.

"Yeah, you ought to work for Homeland Security," she quipped.

"You mean the FBI," I corrected her. "I turned them down."

"They must have been devastated."

"Lana, what that guy told you is bullshit. Aaron is a con-artist."

"Right," she responded while scanning her ticket and entering the station.

I scanned my monthly pass and followed, "Plus, he's probably married with kids."

"Thanks for your opinions," she said disingenuously while walking down the steps towards the platform.

"Men are only as faithful as their options," I continued.

"Shocking Daniel, thank you for the earth-shattering revelation."

"I'm just trying to be helpful."

"Thanks, but I need to go," Lana said while walking further down the platform to get away from me.

I chased after her, and declared, "Do you know what you need?"

"I'm sure you'll tell me."

"Someone who makes you laugh."

"If you find that person, give him my number."

Abruptly I asked, "Lana, why did you stand me up that

day?"

"What?"

"You agreed to meet me back in 2009."

Thinking for a moment, Lana finally answered, "I agreed to have coffee with you, but you deliberately gave me strange directions."

"Why do you say *deliberate*?"

"Your goal was to exhaust and confuse me."

"Nah, you've got it all wrong."

"Your games are a real turnoff," Lana said, as she jumped onto the subway that had arrived.

"Batman, just keep telling yourself that," I shouted angrily. "You're no different from any other chick. You love games."

Locals strolled by, looked me up and down, and laughed. In Mandarin, they whispered, "Crazy foreigner."

CHAPTER 23
Lana Hayaak

The day after the office party, I woke with a splitting headache. As I walked through the living room on my way to the kitchen, I noticed that Curt had left his laptop open on the glass dining table. He must have left in such a hurry that he forgot to close it. This was unusual for him.

On my way back from the kitchen, I gasped because Peter was hovering over my husband's computer. His furry tail was stuck in the air, while he aggressively tore off keys. Peter ripped out the letters H, U, and N with the determination of a lion picking flesh from the bones of a dead gazelle.

I knew I should stop Peter, but my hands were full since I was trying to balance my glass of orange juice in one hand and scalding hot coffee in the other. "Ha, ha, serves you right, Curt." I was still angry over what had transpired last night. So, I returned to my bedroom to focus on getting ready.

I pulled out my train ticket to double check the details. I was supposed to meet Aaron in the First Class cabin at 4:30 p.m. It would be a four-and-a-half hour journey to Beijing on the high-speed train.

I took my time getting dressed since I didn't need to leave for a few hours. I organized important files on various flash drives and carefully packed a thin purse with items such as my passport, USB charger, and money. Then, I prepared a small shoulder bag.

***

I arrived at the expansive *Hongqiao* station early. I found our seats and waited for what seemed like an inordinate amount of time. The train was about to depart when Aaron finally appeared.

He casually approached, removed his suit jacket, and took a seat opposite of me."

"I almost thought you weren't coming," I confessed while observing the intricate tattoos that covered his well-defined arms.

"Would that have upset you?" Aaron asked.

"Not in the least," I insisted.

"Are you sure?" he teased while summoning the waiter and ordering a glass of scotch.

"Isn't it early to drink?"

"Lana, it's almost 5 p.m."

"Fine, I'll have a vodka tonic."

It felt early, but I realized that the sky was already black. The train was now charging into what felt like outer space. We might as well have been voyaging to a distant planet.

Aaron studied my face carefully. "You're not the same person I first met."

I shrugged. "A lot has happened."

Aaron opined, "You were stronger back then."

Startled I asked, "What do you mean?"

"You had fire."

I snapped, "You hardly know me."

Aaron laughed. "I know more about you than anyone."

"You wish," I quipped.

Aaron leaned forward and whispered, "Tell me the truth Lana … you're a drone, aren't you?"

"What are you talking about?" I demanded.

Aaron's hazel eyes flickered with amusement as he downed his scotch and said, "Don't play coy, Lana."

"I'm not playing—"

"I know about the things you've done."

I took a deep breath, adopted a more feminine demeanor, and implored, "Please, what can you tell me about my parents?"

Aaron relaxed, started a new drink, and shared, "Your parents were DEA."

"How do you know?" I asked suspiciously.

"My partner was Special Forces during Vietnam. After the war, he continued to work on covert missions including one that involved your dad."

"Who is your partner?"

"Doesn't matter. Point is, Jason Canaan was corrupt."

"I don't think so," I said flippantly.

"Yes you do. After all, you are your father's daughter."

I shook my head. "This is personal for your partner."

Aaron continued, "Jason sacrificed his entire unit to save himself."

"Based on what evidence?" I demanded.

"One credible witness, Troy."

"Your father is hardly a reliable witness."

"Hey, how did you know Troy is my dad?" Aaron became fully alert, sat upright, and clenched his fists.

"Just my gut."

Aaron ignored my points and continued, "Jason was smart and spoke Vietnamese. When he was taken hostage by the Viet Cong, he shared military secrets that resulted in the capture and torture of his platoon."

I thought about the case, "*Queen v. Dudley, Stephens.*" Was Dad like those defendants? Did he sacrifice his men to save himself? Or was Aaron lying?

"Jason was decorated a hero, got an education, and lived a cushy life," Aaron said.

I nodded to encourage his candor.

"But Jason wanted more," Aaron continued.

"Sure, Dad was very ambitious," I agreed.

"So he made deals and accepted bribes, just like in Vietnam."

"Again, what evidence?"

Aaron leaned back, smiled, and asserted, "Motive is everything."

"Sure," I conceded.

"Why do you think your parents vanished into thin air?"

"They made powerful enemies," I suggested.

Aaron raised an eyebrow and said, "C'mon Lana, that sounds rather conspiratorial, doesn't it?"

"You have no evidence, yet you think I'm conspiratorial?"

Aaron put a finger to his lips and cautioned, "Lana, please lower your voice. People are starting to stare."

Furious, I shouted, "How dare you hush me. I'll start screaming if you don't give me straight answers."

"Not with that attitude."

"Fuck you, Aaron."

Aaron was now laughing.

I lowered my voice and said, "Look I'm sorry my father wasn't as honorable as yours, but what do you want from me?"

Aaron relaxed and confessed, "Dad is no saint."

"At least you've still got one."

"Not really."

"What do you mean?"

"Dad's mind is going …"

"I know it seems unfair that my father survived the POW camps better than others, but some of the Viet Cong were easier on people of color."

"Oh, yeah?" Aaron asked skeptically.

"Some of the educated communists recognized that blacks had been oppressed by the same types who colonized Vietnam."

"Jason Canaan wasn't black."

"True. Dad was Asian like your mother."

"Mom was Japanese," Aaron shared.

"Was?"

"She died, shortly before I met you."

"Sorry to hear that."

"When we met, you were so easy to talk to."

"How much do you know about the history of Japan and Korea?" I asked cautiously.

Aaron shrugged. "Didn't learn much about Asia in Texas, and Mom didn't talk about the past."

"Texas? Your accent is Midwestern." I deliberately changed the subject.

"I was born in Detroit, but moved around a lot."

"I'll bet."

"Didn't you get some big inheritance?"

"Nope."

"There was some house —"

"My cousin got it."

"Yeah, but there was life insurance."

"Sure, but …"

FLASHBACK — 2005

Dad's attorney, sat in his Portland office against a beveled window.

"Natalia, I regret to inform you that there's barely any money left."

"What?" I asked in a shaky voice.

"Your father never paid the taxes."

"But Dad only received a life-estate."

"Correct, but your father was responsible for the property taxes."

"So there's nothing left?" I exclaimed.

"After my fees and the interest on the arrearages, you'll have a few

thousand dollars."

Aaron intently listened as I described what transpired. Finally, he said, "Dad said you got some major insurance settlement."

"I was in a car accident when I was twenty-three."

"You look fine, so what happened?"

"I didn't have insurance, but a personal injury attorney called the driver's insurance company and negotiated a decent settlement. He hinted that a new statute could make him liable."

"Must have been a good settlement," Aaron remarked snidely.

"It barely covered my medical expenses."

"Uh, huh."

"So money is the reason you lured me out here?"

"Not exactly," Aaron replied as he downed more whiskey.

"You're a contractor, aren't you?" I asked.

"How did you know?"

I didn't, but you keep confirming my assumptions.

"I know who hired you," I bluffed.

"Oh, yeah?"

"Yes."

"Cool, I'd like to know, because even Dad doesn't."

"So you both work for private contractors?"

"Yep, mostly security stuff."

"The client is probably …" I hesitated while thinking of what to say. Finally, I suggested, "My husband must have hired you."

"Lana, I told you that I have no idea."

I continued, "Curt is testing me."

Aaron shook his head and said, "That sounds weird. Who would do that?"

"We signed an agreement whereby if I commit adultery, I'm not entitled to any money Curt makes while we're married. There's this upcoming deal —"

"What do you see in Steiger, anyway?"

"It's hard to explain."

"Since when are you at a loss for words?"

"We were in law school together —"

Aaron shook his head, dismissing my explanation. "You're an illusion to Steiger."

"Why do you say that?"

"How much does Curt know about you?"

"More than you think."

"Yeah, right."

"Curt might not know me well, but I understand him."

"Why would you understand a German chemist?"

"Most of my childhood memories are of Berlin."

"Yeah, but Steiger is from Stuttgart."

Out of patience, I snapped, "Why do you care so much about my marriage?"

Aaron chuckled. "I don't, but based on your behavior it's obvious that you've got a lot of issues."

"My behavior?"

"Yeah, you're on a train with me and headed to Beijing knowing your parents aren't there."

I nodded and murmured absent-mindedly, "Curt and I have friends."

Aaron shook his head, looked me straight in the eye and said, "Lana, you've got no friends."

I took a deep breath, and digested the drunken man's advice.

"I need to go," I said. As I stood up, Aaron attempted to stop me, but he was extremely sluggish thanks to the sleeping pill I had slipped him earlier. He quickly passed out.

I collected my things, charged towards the doors, and jumped off the train, which had briefly stopped to refuel.

As I ran into the middle of China, I thought about things. I had long suspected that the drug my husband was working on was not a success.

I didn't know much about pharmaceutics, but I was familiar with issues faced by startups. A company could falsify preclinical data and sell it to an unsuspecting company. However, I had no evidence and besides — would anyone even care?

As I wandered through the fog, I thought about an old film: *Shanghai Gesture*. The opening line was, "There are no heroes in Shanghai. There are only predators and survivors."

"Daniel is wrong," I whispered. "I'm no Batman. I'm no hero, nor do I aspire to be one."

I ran into the dark night, where not even the moon or stars provided light. The cold air penetrated my clothing, and I felt chills run through my bones. I shivered as a rash of goosebumps erupted across my arms. I held my bag closely as if I was cradling a baby.

CHAPTER 27

Meanwhile, back in Shanghai, Curt was fatigued from running at one hundred percent for so many weeks.

When he got home, he stumbled in the dark because none of the lights were on. Curt didn't hear Lana on the phone, typing, or watching *Russia Today* as he usually did.

Curt repeatedly shouted, "Lana? Where are you?"

He figured that his wife was at an event or avoiding him because of last night's ordeal. Curt thought she would be angry for a few days, but would eventually get over it.

It didn't occur to Curt that Lana had gone to meet Aaron, because the driver and staff had been instructed to keep a close eye on her. No one had reported anything out of the ordinary. What Curt didn't know was that Lana had drugged both the driver and security guard with gourmet food that neither could resist.

Curt crossed the living room and saw his laptop on the dining table. "Why is this open?" he shouted. When he saw three keys scattered across the floor, he stammered, "What the hell?" Then he yelled, "Peter, you stupid cat, where are you? I'm going to kill you!"

Curt kicked the dishes on the kitchen floor, not realizing

that both bowls were empty. Lana always left water and dry food out for her pet.

Curt frantically searched the apartment for Peter by looking under the bed, couch, table, and closets until he realized the cat was gone.

He called Lana's cell number several times, but discovered her line was disconnected.

The reception desk reported seeing Lana leave around 1:30 p.m. She wore a popular trench coat worn by millions of women in China. Plus, she carried a small bag that was large enough to fit a cat. The staff didn't think anything was out of the ordinary.

Curt called all of Lana's friends, but no one had any idea where she was. Finally, he called Ben, who rushed over immediately even though it was the middle of the night.

"Where is she? All of her things are here: clothing, jewelry, and shoes. The only thing missing is Peter."

"Don't worry Curt. We'll find her because it's impossible to disappear in China."

CHAPTER 28

A few days later, a Shanghai police detective visited Curt who was visibly sleep-deprived. While the two spoke in the dining room, Ben listened.

"Your wife was last seen jumping off a train two hours outside of Beijing."

"Why was she there?"

Ben interjected, "Lana believed Aaron's story about her parents in Beijing."

Curt snapped, "Did she run off with that guy?"

"We've looked into that. Mr. Walker is back in *Guangzhou* with his wife and children," the detective replied. He paused before saying, "He wishes to press charges against your wife."

"What?" Curt exclaimed.

"Apparently, Mrs. Steiger drugged Mr. Walker, after he had four glasses of whiskey. He insists we charge her with attempted murder."

"Are you serious?"

The detective responded, "In China, we take crimes very seriously. However, right now our primary focus is finding your wife."

"Have you checked Beijing?" Curt asked.

"We've investigated all over China. So far, we can't locate her anywhere. Official ID is required for travel," the detective responded.

"What about the airports?"

"There's no record of her, or any woman matching her description."

"She must have taken the cat with her."

"It's not easy to take a cat out of this country. It requires a health certificate and a lot of paperwork," the detective stated.

"Maybe she left another way," Curt suggested.

"We've set up checkpoints for buses and cars throughout the country," the detective continued.

Curt stared out the window and lamented, "We have to find my wife because she can't survive without me. She can't even read a map."

"Don't worry, we'll find her," Ben assured his friend.

"Lana is vulnerable and emotionally fragile," Curt continued.

"Your wife is like a peach. She's soft on the outside, but has a strong core," Ben reassured his friend.

CHAPTER 29
November 2015

Kamlesh Khan sat at his cubicle in the IT department of Curt's Shanghai office. He finally discovered that the password to Lana's email account was her cat's adoption date, which was also Curt Steiger's birthday.

Kamlesh wasn't pleased with this hacking assignment because he knew how much Lana valued privacy.

After hours of research, he printed dozens of emails, as well as a police report from Oregon.

Meanwhile Curt sat in his office and stared at his computer. Upon seeing Kamlesh briskly enter, he looked up and asked, "Hey, what'd you find?"

"Dozens of emails from some lunatic," Kamlesh responded, as he handed a stack of paper to Curt.

"Yuck," said the distraught husband, as he rifled through selfies of Cal in his underwear. "This must be the guy who kidnapped her?"

Kamlesh shook his head and said, "I immediately followed up by calling the police department in Portland."

"Khan, I'm impressed by your initiative. I wondered why my wife was friends with a tech guy, but you're more than a geek. You're a detective."

"Thanks," the hacker sighed. "Unfortunately, this guy didn't have anything to do with Lana's disappearance."

"How do you know?"

"Cal spent the last month in an Oregon prison."

"For what?"

"He burned down the house where Lana lived."

"I didn't know she lived in Oregon."

Kamlesh wondered, *Didn't you ever ask her any questions?*

"Was it arson?"

Kamlesh shook his head. "Nah, it was an accident. Cal and his friends broke into the vacant house. They threw a party, and some candles tipped over."

Abruptly changing the subject, Curt asked, "Did you get a hold of her gay friend?"

"You mean Eric?"

"Sure."

"He quit his job and returned to D.C. The office party, with Lana, was his last day in Shanghai. He hasn't returned any of my calls or emails."

CHAPTER 30
2017

Lana had been missing for almost two years. In 2016, Curt returned to the Bay Area with his partner Ben.

Daniel's clothes were a mess. He looked worn and disheveled while sitting in the Shanghai police department. His dark beard was overgrown, and he smelled of liquor, from a recent excursion.

Daniel stammered while reading a photocopied diary entry, which was covered in beer-stains:

"Dear Diary,

Yesterday, I was sitting at a café near my apartment. I was finishing my coffee when I looked up and saw a frail old man ravenously eating a plate of abandoned donuts. I was shocked because I hadn't seen this before.

My home is coddled away from the horrors of the world. The man was appallingly thin, his skin was tough like leather, and he ate with such intensity. I glanced at the counter and realized that the clerk had caught me staring. Thus, she demanded that the man leave. If I hadn't been staring, this wouldn't have happened.

The man ran across the street. I followed and gave him my hot coffee. He accepted it, smiled and said 'Xiè, Xie,' repeatedly. He owed me no gratitude. After all, I was responsible for getting him tossed from the café."

The detective listened patiently but finally interrupted. "Thank you for sharing, but what is your point?"

"Lana was a nice person."

"I know," the detective responded flippantly while finishing his cigarette. He then leaned forward and asked, "Is there anything in *that* diary remotely relevant to this investigation?"

"Not exactly, but you can infer who had the incentive to murder her."

"Infer?"

"Curt made a lot of money. Lana would have gotten half of it."

"Wasn't he your employer?"

"Curt was my client. He hired me to follow his wife."

"I see."

"The guy was never honest about anything. Plus, he left China so abruptly."

"Where were you when the *tai tai* disappeared?"

"Huh?"

"Weren't you supposed to follow her?"

"Yeah, but I got sick."

"I see," responded the detective stoically.

"Um, yeah, I passed out after consuming —"

"Mrs. Steiger's train didn't leave until *after* 4 p.m. Why were you drinking in the afternoon?"

"I wasn't. An admirer left a basket of caviar and chocolate for me. I ate all of it and fell asleep."

"Admirer?" the detective asked with disbelief.

"Yeah," Daniel replied smiling. "I'm popular with the ladies."

"I see."

"I'm debonair."

"Obviously," the detective lied. "So who was *this* admirer?"

"Some gal at the women's club, Mrs. Gloria Rivers."

"Did you verify that?"

"Nah, the old doll has been after me for years. Who else could it have been?"

The detective exhaled and said cordially, "We appreciate your interest, but this case is closed."

"Why? Lana is still missing."

"Yes, she's missing, but there's no trace of her. She's probably dead."

"Lana was murdered by her husband. Arrest him."

"Without a body, it's impossible to charge anyone. Steiger has a solid alibi, and he was genuinely grief-stricken over her disappearance."

"Yeah, the guy has a guilty conscience," Daniel suggested sarcastically.

"Mr. Petersen, I'm sorry to change the subject …"

The detective paused briefly to light a new cigarette. He offered one to Daniel who shook his head.

The detective continued, "We're well aware that you're working in China without a business visa."

"What?" Daniel said with alarm.

"The government is clamping down on these violations."

"Hey, are you threatening me?"

"You need to leave. I advise that you either get a proper work permit or stop working in China."

Daniel got up and left without saying anything.

Later, a different detective entered and asked, "Was it that *lao wai* again?"

"Yep, he's relentless."

"So Mr. Petersen followed Mrs. Steiger for weeks, but never learned much, did he?"

"He was useless."

"Yes, and all we have is gossip by the local staff."

"Sure, and we don't know if any of it is true. It's speculation based on the fact that Ben Chang entered Mrs. Steiger's apartment when she was alone. The two were then seen at a restaurant with another foreigner."

"Steiger probably asked Chang to check on her."

"Yes, so this case is closed."

"Maybe Mrs. Steiger crossed the border and made her way to Russia."

"We may never know."

PART 5
SILICON VALLEY — 2022-2023

CHAPTER 1
2022

Curt and Ben had been back in Silicon Valley for almost six years. The partners left Shanghai less than a year after the unexplained disappearance of Lana.

Curt and Ben succeeded in selling the drug program that exhausted them for years. Luckily for both, the company that purchased the flawed drug never tested it on any humans. The purchaser's ultimate goal was to eliminate competition against their own similar program. Thus, the partners avoided getting caught and charged with fraud.

The millions gained by the sale drove up the company's stock price, which made Curt an instant millionaire. He invested his money wisely, started a venture capital firm, and became a billionaire.

For years, Curt imagined seeing his wife everywhere. During business trips to San Diego, Zurich, and Toronto, he frequently left meetings to chase after women who resembled his wife.

CHAPTER 2

Despite the warm weather and rays of sun that beamed through the windows, Curt was in a bad mood. Formerly a controlled man, losing his temper had become routine. He sat in his Palo Alto office, furiously working to complete a new project that he regretted undertaking.

Curt spoke sharply to Priya Patel, a new chemist who wore thin, wire-rimmed glasses around her piercing dark eyes, which were adorned by thick lashes. She was a petite woman, but hardly a pushover.

Ben avoided direct conflict with Curt but was losing patience with his ornery partner, because they couldn't retain good scientists. Ben was desperate to prevent Priya from quitting.

"Let's get out and grab a drink," Ben suggested. "We can drive to a nearby watering hole."

As Priya climbed into the passenger's seat of Ben's Tesla, she said, "I don't understand why someone so successful is so angry."

Ben drove cautiously through the sunny yet shaded streets of University Avenue. He responded, "We greatly value your expertise and don't want to lose you."

Priya didn't say anything during the brief drive, because she was lost in thought. When Ben pulled into the parking lot of a local pub, the young scientist confessed, "I'm not sure whether I want to stay. Steiger is exceptionally difficult."

Ben nodded, as the two walked into the pub and took seats at the counter. "Curt Steiger wasn't always like this."

"Seriously?" Priya asked with disbelief.

Ben ordered beers from the bartender and then explained to Priya, "Curt seems rough and can be harsh towards new chemists, but that's only in the beginning. Once you get to know him, he's a great guy."

"That's hard to believe," Priya remarked as she took a tiny sip. She didn't like beer and rarely drank alcohol.

"Curt changed when his wife disappeared."

"Yeah, I've heard the stories. They never found his wife?"

"Nope, she vanished into thin air," Ben said as he drank his beer.

"How is that even possible?"

"In China, it's extremely difficult for a foreigner to disappear, but Lana managed the unthinkable."

"It's been years. Has Curt finally accepted that she's gone?"

Ben shook his head. "He believes that she's alive and out there somewhere. Curt's mind is stuck in 2015. That's when they both lived in Shanghai."

Priya nodded. "Hope is the worst of all evils because it prolongs the torments of man."

"Well, I hate to disagree with Nietzsche, but there's something far worse than hope."

"What?" asked Priya with piqued curiosity.

"Betrayal," Ben declared bitterly.

CHAPTER 3

In late October, Ben marched into his partner's office and said, "Sorry to interrupt, but you need to sign these."

Curt quickly rifled through the documents and hurled them into the trash can. He shouted, "No, I won't sign those damn papers."

"Signing them doesn't mean Lana is dead. It's simply a formality. After all, it's been seven years."

Curt shook his head.

Ben continued, "This will allow you to collect on the life insurance policy that you took out on her in 2014."

Curt grumbled, "I don't need or want the money."

"You could start a foundation in Lana's name or give it to charity. She would have wanted that," Ben suggested.

"Huh?"

"Donate the half million to a cause focused on animal welfare, the elderly, children, or the disabled. These are all causes that Lana supported."

Curt gazed out of the window and mumbled, "Why did she do this to me?"

Ben didn't say anything.

"Why did she leave me? Not a single word. No note, no

explanation … nothing. Lana didn't even want my money, because she didn't take a dime."

Ben had stopped responding to Curt's questions years ago. There was nothing anyone could say or do to stop Steiger's obsessive behavior. Secretly, Ben felt they went too far with the spying. If they had left Lana alone, she would have been happier. On the other hand, she always seemed like a person who would depart at any moment.

"Curt, if you sign these papers, then you can remarry," Ben said.

"I don't want to."

"But you and Cindy have been living together for years. She wants to get married."

"Yeah, she's always wanted to marry me," Curt agreed smugly.

"Cindy has been a great comfort to you," Ben reminded his friend.

Abruptly changing the subject Curt asked, "Did you know my mother wasn't from the West?"

Ben was used to erratic remarks from his partner, so he simply responded, "I thought your mother was German."

"Yeah, but she escaped from East Berlin when she was a teenager."

"Your mother was a lovely woman."

"Mom never talked about her past, but I always felt like there were stories she wanted to share, but couldn't."

Ben nodded. "Kind of like Lana."

CHAPTER 4
2023

Curt and Cindy's wedding, held at a vineyard in Sonoma, was extravagant and attended by many of Silicon Valley's leading players.

The groom sat at the head table next to his best man Ben. The bride beamed with contentment while wearing an ornate white wedding gown that was excessive for a woman her age.

During dinner, she laughed happily and chatted with guests.

"I think a strong Asian upbringing is necessary for producing successful children," Cindy boasted.

Guests throughout the room nodded politely.

The bride continued, "When I was growing up, I got the wooden spoon, the belt, or the end of a shoe horn as punishment."

Priya sat at a table with staff from Curt's company. She paused when she heard Cindy's declaration and thought, *why extrapolate something positive from something routinely shown to produce ineffective results?*

Cindy's maid of honor Amy wore a baroque, plum-colored gown. Enthusiastically she jumped up and grabbed the microphone. Standing before the hall filled with wedding guests, Amy gushed, "I've known Cindy for most of my life. She's like a sister. All I've ever wanted was the best for her, and the best is marrying Curt."

The audience clapped.

Amy then asked, "Do you all believe in fairy tales?"

Curt, Ben, and scientists throughout the room cringed.

"Do we believe in fairy tales? Is she serious?" Priya whispered to Kamlesh.

"I believe in fucking nightmares," Curt muttered under his breath, but no one heard him.

Amy continued, "The relationship between Curt and Cindy is like a magical fairy tale. It's like *Cinderella, Romeo and Juliet*, or Taylor Swift's 'Love Story.'"

Someone in the audience whispered, "What Christmas tree did that fruitcake fall off of? Doesn't Amy know that *Romeo and Juliet* was about innocent teenagers?"

After Amy finished her toast, Cindy worked the room by eagerly chatting with guests. Meanwhile, the groom didn't bother to get up. Curt paid little attention to the wedding around him. Instead, he thought about Lana when they were young.

Having consumed too much champagne, Curt passed out and dreamt that he was back in law school.

FLASHBACK – 2008

On his way back from the library, Curt sat down at a table where Lana was studying. She looked up and asked, "What do you think about IP law?"

"It's my focus. Why?"

"I don't believe in ownership," she asserted boldly.

Curt laughed and said, "Then you picked the wrong place to live."

"Why do you support patent law?"

"It furthers innovation."

"Does it, really? There's no patent law for fashion or cuisine, yet

those industries flourish."

"Yeah, it's 'rich man's poker,' because only the super wealthy can play, especially in my industry … pharma."

As Curt slept, he felt someone shaking him.

"Curt, wake up! Wake up right now. You're so rude," his bride exclaimed.

***

In the next room, Priya and Ben talked briefly about an upcoming project. Simultaneously, they observed the wedding from afar.

"I love whiskey," Ben said, reaching for another glass. Priya was shocked by her boss's tolerance for hard alcohol. For such a slender man, he didn't appear drunk, nor did he slur his words.

"You're very happy," Priya noted as she sipped orange juice.

Ben nodded. "I want what is best for Curt."

"Certainly," Priya acknowledged diplomatically.

As if reading her mind, Ben said, "Priya, you have to understand that Cindy is like a coconut. Similar to my wife, she seems hard on the outside, but underneath she's all heart."

"Years ago, I met Lana," Priya suddenly confessed.

"At a pharma event?"

"Yes, she expressed genuine interest in a book about the East India Company, which I edited for my mother, an Oxford-educated Professor of History. We talked for hours."

"Sure, she's quite the dilettante," Ben conceded.

"Dilettante?"

"Lana knows a little bit about everything, which allowed her to be a good host at cocktail parties. However, her knowledge was hardly significant. In fact, it was quite shallow if you scratched the surface."

"Okay, but she was sincere. At one point, Lana stopped to comfort a new pharma rep who was like a lost puppy."

"Sure," Ben agreed.

"The rep was shy and felt out of place."

Changing the subject, Ben asked, "Priya, whom does a chemist marry for life?"

"A good chemist marries her research?"

Ben nodded. "Exactly, a chemist can only ever truly have one wife: his work."

Priya listened while Ben continued, "Cindy is loyal and won't cause problems like Lana."

"What problems?"

"One time, Lana showed up at Curt's office demanding to know if we tested on animals, what types, and how."

Priya's eyes widened since she loved animals.

Ben continued, "Another time, Lana demanded to know what one of our investors meant when he said, 'China is a great place to set up experiments because they lack the West's Judeo-Christian values.'"

"What did he mean?" Priya asked.

Ben ignored her and said, "It was a dumb thing for the investor to say publicly, but Lana wouldn't let up."

"Let up?"

"Lana kept messaging me to find out if this investor was trying to create biomedical weaponry for the U.S. military."

"Are you serious?"

"Yeah, Lana was convinced that the military was funding some of this investor's projects."

Well, was he? Priya wanted to ask, but she refrained.

"The woman had a very wild imagination," Ben complained.

***

Ben returned to his table while Priya walked into the rose garden, where Kamlesh sat alone on a bench watching water trickle from a Spanish-style fountain. He gripped a dessert plate in his hands. It was stacked high with pastel-colored macaroons.

"Aren't you supposed to eat the entire cookie before moving to the next?" Priya teased.

"Nah, it's better this way," Kamlesh replied while taking individual bites out of each macaroon before tossing them aside.

"You were Lana's friend, weren't you?" she asked while sitting down next to him.

Kamlesh nodded. "We talked about everything: tech, politics, and re-runs of our favorite show, *Desperate Housewives*."

Changing the subject, Priya asked, "Ben is the alpha in this company, isn't he?"

"Yep, that's why there were problems when Lana asked Curt if she could be on the board of directors."

"Lana wanted to be on the board?"

"Yep and she wouldn't have been passive."

"Apparently not."

"Yeah, Lana had a lot of progressive ideas regarding employee rights."

"That's great."

"Yep, fewer work hours, longer vacations, and active participation in management."

"How nice."

"Yep," Kamlesh agreed.

"So, what's Cindy's connection with Ben?"

"They're cousins and are descended from some Chinese Diaspora. They can trace their roots back to the 7th century."

Priya looked surprised and responded, "But I thought Cindy was Cantonese."

"Her mom is Cantonese, but her dad and Ben's father are some other type. I can't remember what they're called, but it's a very secretive group."

"Sounds mysterious."

"Yeah, rumor has it their ancestors were drug dealers and money launderers."

Priya nodded. "But now they both work in big pharma."

"Yep, Ben went to MIT, but during breaks, he always returned home to Fremont."

"I thought Ben went to Stanford," Priya interjected.

"Ben transferred after he met Curt through Cindy."

"Okay."

"Neither Cindy nor Curt were originally from the Bay Area, so Ben's family adopted both of them. The three quickly became best friends."

Priya paused for a second, but then said, "Ben gave me the impression that Curt is still in love with his former wife."

Kamlesh snorted. "Ha! Ben is quite the charmer. He figured that a romantic story about Curt and Lana would make you sympathetic to your new boss. But mostly Ben was trying to distract you from the truth."

"The truth?" Priya asked with concern.

"Curt has overextended himself. His VC has taken on way too many projects."

"That sounds serious."

"Yeah, which is why Curt is wound so tight, and Cindy needs to be on board."

"I heard Curt brag that Cindy has always been in love with him."

Kamlesh shook his head furiously and declared, "When it comes to non-science matters, forget what Steiger says."

"Okay," Priya agreed.

"According to Amy, Curt practically stalked Cindy when they were at Stanford. Lots of guys were after her, so when he broke up with her, she was devastated."

"She'd never been dumped before?"

"Nope, Cindy moved on and got engaged to someone else. But her parents were furious when they discovered that her fiancée was broke."

"Parents are like that."

"After Lana disappeared, Cindy started getting messages from Ben, begging her to return to the company. He insisted that the company needed her."

"Why?"

"Curt may be a good scientist, but Cindy is a natural-born leader. She'll move this company forward."

"What's it like working for Cindy?" Priya asked.

"She comes off as cold, but she's fair and rewards loyalty."

"Isn't your friendship with Lana a breach of your loyalty to her?"

"Nah, Cindy is too professional to care."

"That's good."

Kamlesh continued, "I loved Lana, but her stories were … fanciful."

"Like how?" Priya asked.

Kamlesh lowered his voice and whispered, "She told a tale about Cindy that involved cocaine."

"Really?" Priya exclaimed.

"Yep, and you can imagine how Ben felt about that."

"He must have been angry."

"Very," Kamlesh responded.

EPILOGUE

SHANGHAI — 2015
(Six hours before Curt's office party)

Déjà vu hit me as I entered the lobby, which made sense since I'd been to this venue in the past. However, today's nostalgia was unrelated to any party or event that I'd attended in Shanghai.

I walked past the reception desk and took the elevator to the 14th floor. While wandering through the hallways, my thoughts flickered back to 2009.

I suddenly heard, "*Nín yǒu shé me xūyào bāngmáng de ma?*"

Abruptly, I woke from my daydream and realized I was lost.

"*Bù yòng xiè,*" I responded to an attendant who stood politely at the far end of a dark corridor. I scolded myself for being so careless because I didn't want to run into anyone who might identify me. I touched my head to ensure that my bob-style wig was still intact.

I crept carefully to room 1408 and slowly knocked. I waited quietly in the hallway and listened to powerful steps approach. The door swung wide open. Kevin grinned and said, "I knew you'd come."

I entered the room, removed my dark sunglasses, and noted, "This is a single and not a suite."

Kevin responded, "Yep, thanks for stating the obvious."

I said nothing, but critically observed the lack of a living room.

Kevin chuckled, "Well, I'm sorry this isn't up to your usual standards."

"That's hardly the issue. If anything, this hotel is rather excessive, don't you think?"

"Why do you care?" Kevin asked.

I was about to say something but stopped. I paused for a moment and then declared, "Look I'm in enough trouble as it is. People are always scrutinizing me. Think about how this looks."

"That's not my problem," Kevin said flippantly.

"Yes, it is. It's our problem, surely you could have —"

Kevin looked irritated and snapped, "Lana, I don't make the rules. I'm just a —"

"Cog in a wheel," I finished.

Kevin stared at me for a moment, before correcting me: "paid professional."

"I don't have a lot of time," I said, while taking a seat at the desk by the window.

"Are you sure about that, Mrs. Steiger?"

"Ms. Hayaak," I corrected him curtly.

Kevin snorted. "Ms. Hayaak, it seems like you have all the time in the world. What's it like being a housewife?"

"I am not a housewife," I protested with heavy irritation, "I am —"

"Quite the socialite," Kevin joked.

"Sure. I'm a lady of leisure who sleeps 'til noon and subsists on a diet of Manhattans while lounging around eating bonbons."

"Now that's the spirit, Lana."

I stared out the window, and remarked, "Don't you think it's a bit cruel to drag my parents into things?"

"Who do you think we are? The boy scouts?"

"Why mention my parents?"

Kevin shrugged. "It gives you an easy out."

"I don't want to use my parents as an explanation for anything."

"Hey, honey, we don't care what you say, but it's your responsibility to protect your identity. You've known that from the start." Kevin was getting impatient with me. "Now let's hurry up and get this over with, so that you can get back to your ... *important life*."

I was too agitated to respond, but I heard him say, "Shall we begin?"

"Yes, I was born —"

"No, not that far back, please take this seriously and be professional."

I took a deep breath and asserted, "But I've said all that can be possibly said. What more could you people possibly want to know?"

"Us people, Lana?"

"I meant ..." I stammered.

"Alright then, begin in 2010."

"It was mid-October of 2010 when I finished training. It had been a long, hot summer and my reward was a plane ticket to Libya. I had never deluded myself. Back in 2008, when 'George' said I would get sent to Paris or Santiago, I figured it was one of those recruitment promises that would never actualize."

Kevin said nothing and scrutinized my body language. I bit my tongue to keep from compressing my lips. I reached for a glass of water and sipped too slowly. I felt awkward discussing my personal life. I was accustomed to superficial conversations.

I was a good listener, curious by nature, and could remember the tiniest details about anyone I'd ever met. I suspected that this was not the case for my current interrogator. He was merely following procedures designed to ascertain inconsistencies within my story.

"Libya was a dream," I continued, *"an unimaginable paradise that surpassed my expectations."*

Kevin raised an eyebrow in disbelief.

"At least, before the civil war began. My expectations had been low, and I thought I would end up in a less desirable location despite promises made during the elaborate interview process. Libya wasn't London or Paris, but it was exotic and full of opportunity. After all, it was the second wealthiest country in all of Africa, thanks to oil and gas."

"Sure, but what about your life back home?" Kevin asked.

"I didn't have one. I had no family, no parents, no —"

"No husband or fiancée?" Kevin asked.

"Nope, I had no commitments whatsoever. I didn't even have a cat. The only thing I owned was debt — and plenty of it."

Kevin nodded.

"The Libyan Civil War began in mid-February of 2011. When I started in 2010, it was the calm before the storm."

"Why did they send you?" Kevin asked.

"You've read my file, haven't you?"

"I need to hear what happened in your words. Please stop wasting time with questions."

"When I arrived in Tripoli, there were a lot of new construction projects underway. These included luxury hotels and convention centers for the Government of Libya. New investment laws had opened this Arab market to the world."

Kevin interrupted to say, "You didn't answer the

question."

"I was sent to Libya as a new associate with Ares Venture Capital from Silicon Valley since there were plenty of opportunities for private investments. Construction sites and half-built towers dotted the skyline when I began. Foreign investment was apparent from the different languages such as Korean that were stamped out on development sites."

I paused to drink from a glass of water before continuing. I observed my lipstick stain with disdain. Kevin looked at me impatiently.

"At the time, Tripoli was a city alive with possibility. As I descended the stairs from the plane into this scorching hot country surrounded by desert, it seemed like a place with endless potential.

My apartment was clean, modern, and near the financial center where I worked. However, I soon learned that the life of a new associate was far from glamorous."

Kevin listened as I continued talking.

"Daily, I walked through the dry, dusty city to get to my office, in part for the exercise, but also because I was eager to soak up as much of the culture as I possibly could. I woke daily to the sound of the call to prayer, which reminded me of Istanbul. I think I liked Libya because it felt familiar."

I continued my monologue, occasionally pausing in case Kevin wished to interject.

"The reception where I worked was cold, but I anticipated that. Upon arrival, I was met by an older woman named Bonnie. She was kind, gave me my security pass, and assigned me to a back room in the basement of the office building. Bonnie explained that the Vice Presidents of the firm were away on business and wouldn't be back

anytime soon. She reminded me not to have any interaction with the U.S. Embassy. These were the instructions I had received numerous times. I entered my office with enthusiasm, but soon felt assaulted by the sheer volume of documents I was expected to review."

"What types of documents?" Kevin asked.

"There were many different types that had been thrown into boxes without any semblance of logic. I was tasked with creating some type of filing system."

"Sounds very clerical," Kevin remarked.

"Sure; however, understanding the language of these documents was pertinent to the job. There were many types: non-disclosure agreements, building contracts, and exploration licenses awarded to various Western companies."

"Western companies?" Kevin asked.

"Yes, British, French, and even some American companies."

Kevin scribbled notes on his pad.

"During the day, I reviewed documents in isolation. For lunch the receptionist ordered North African food. I ate my bazin with chickpeas and hot peppers alone. I had expected a heavy schedule of nighttime commitments; however, Bonnie assigned nothing.

In the evening, I returned to an empty apartment and watched Al Jazeera news which reported:

'Libya is demanding political concessions in return for business deals. Officials stress they don't need capital. What they need is technical and management expertise. In other words, Libya is not a place for short-term returns because the government takes a long-term approach and prefers deals based on mutual interest. The government wants cooperation based on partnerships with large companies, in a way that isn't about implementing contracts, but building consistency and sustainability.'"

Kevin interrupted, "I don't need the info dump."

I continued,

"One Friday night, I was finishing work when a colleague, Rick, a young associate, popped his head into my office and asked, 'Lana, what are your plans for tonight?'

I was packing up my things and said 'Nothing really, I thought I would go home and finish reading Jane Eyre.'

'Are you serious?' Rick joked.

'Yes, I'm at a delicious part of the book and —'

'Ha, ha, you're funny. C'mon, let's head over to The Sahara, it's a popular watering hole.'

When we arrived, the place was packed, mostly with men. The room was super smoky. It wasn't long before a group of guys asked us to join them. I didn't learn anything particularly unique. It was the Al Jazeera bite-lines passed around by guys anxious to appear knowledgeable.

I yawned since it was getting late, so Rick offered to take me home. On the way back to my place, I said, 'Rick, I don't understand. Before I arrived, I studied so much about Libya, and it's not what I expected. I thought the government was oppressing its people.'

'There's a whole different side to Libya that you don't see out in the open, Lana.'

'Sure, but from what I can see, there's a high standard of living. In fact, it's better than San Francisco or L.A., where homelessness is rampant.'

Rick responded, 'Yep, Gaddafi does a good job of hiding his poor, but his population is relatively small, and he has a lot of gold in his reserves. 140 billion tons if I'm correct. The U.K. has twice that amount, but they have ten times the population.'

'What do you think about Gaddafi?' I asked.

'Gaddafi has been a very active peacemaker in Chad, Sudan, and Somalia. We need his cooperation in these places. He knows Africa well; however, I don't think he knows this continent well enough. Thus, he needs some adult supervision.'

Rick talked for a while, but I didn't respond because I was put off by his youthful arrogance."

Kevin suddenly interrupted, "What about the uprisings in 2011?"

"Working at Ares office from 8 a.m. until 7 p.m. or later, kept me quite sheltered from everything: drone attacks, Libyan people, and reality. Early in 2011, Libya was faced with a chaotic insurrection, partly inspired by the revolts in Tunisia and Egypt and partly led by Islamic fundamentalists. In March, NATO forces began a bombardment. According to Obama, the intervention was to protect civilians."

Kevin nodded approvingly.

I continued,

"For others, it was about oil and Gaddafi's plan to quit selling his Libyan reserves in U.S. dollars — demanding payment instead in gold-backed —'dinars'."

Kevin's countenance swiftly changed. Aggravated, he snapped, "Let's talk about Peter Lim. You've avoided mentioning him."

I paused and took a long drink of water. "Peter — well, I guess we need to back up a bit."

"Tell me when you met Peter and how your relationship with him developed," Kevin ordered.

I continued,

"I was with Ares Venture Capital for months before the uprising began. Our work was legitimate, and Ares VC was a bona fide company."

"Lana, you're repeating yourself. Stop deflecting and get to the point."

I sighed and began what felt like a long story:

"It was late December, right before the holidays. Most of the ex-pats in the foreign community had left. Rick and Bonnie returned to

the States for Christmas. I remained in Tripoli and stayed late at the office to finish paperwork.

When I got back to my apartment, I hopped into the elevator. As I did, I heard a man yell, 'please hold the elevator!' I hit the 'hold button,' and a tall man with a square jaw and sharp cheekbones jumped on."

Kevin nodded and wrote some notes.

"The man smiled confidently and asked, 'Where are you from?'
'San Francisco,' I replied.
'So you're American?'
'Yes,' I answered, debating whether to ask if he was from China.
'You don't look American,' he observed.
'What do I look like?'
He leaned back against the elevator door and said with amusement, 'You look Arabic.'
'Where are you from?'
'Beijing,' he replied.
Suddenly, the elevator doors opened, and we both stepped out. I was surprised that we shared the same floor. It was awkward, so I said goodnight as quickly as I could and rushed away."

Kevin smirked. I ignored him and continued telling my story.

"A few days later, it was Christmas Eve, and I had an early flight to Dubai. I was sleepy while waiting for the taxi, ordered by the reception desk. When a cab drove up, I raced to the curb, and a tall Arab man said abruptly, 'airport?'

I nodded, and he helped me with my bag. I jumped into the back, relieved to be on my way out of Libya, which now felt like a fishbowl, or as some were fond of saying, 'a Golden Prison.'

The taxi whizzed through the empty streets, and I observed my surroundings with intrigue. I started to doze off but jolted alert when I realized I had no idea where we were going. The taxi was driving more *than 80 miles an hour.*

Startled, I exclaimed, 'Where are we going?'

The very masculine driver was annoyed and shouted something I didn't understand. I ascertained it was the name of another airport.

'What? No, I need to go to the Tripoli Airport,' I protested.

The driver started making phone calls. He was outraged and said, 'You're not the person I was supposed to pick up.'

'Um, okay,' I replied, 'well, can we go to the Tripoli International Airport?'

'No, I have to take you back to your apartment and get my other party. Otherwise, I will be in a lot of trouble.'

I nodded, suddenly feeling sorry for the taxi driver. I technically had more than enough time to make it to the airport, so I rifled through my purse searching for a cash tip to compensate the guy for his trouble.

The return felt long, but in reality, it was only 15 minutes. My heart was racing, as I jumped out of the cab, grabbed my bag, and handed money to the driver. I was scurrying towards a row of taxis when I saw a familiar face. It was the man I met on the elevator.

My cheeks flushed as I exclaimed, 'I'm so sorry, but I accidentally stole your taxi.'

'It's quite alright,' he said nonchalantly. 'Would you like to come with me?'

I laughed and replied, 'Thank you, but I'm on my way to Dubai.'

'That's my destination. My friend has a private jet.'

'Ah, I already paid for my seat on Emirates. If I don't show, then I won't get my miles,' I explained as I hurried away.

The taxi driver smiled and shouted, 'God bless America.'

When I arrived at my hotel in Dubai, who should I see, but my new neighbor. He was sitting in the lobby lounge drinking coffee and reading a newspaper. As I strolled by, he looked up and spotted me. He darted over and said, 'This is quite a coincidence.'

'I guess so,' I replied. I was skeptical because I don't believe in coincidences.

'It's such a small world. Please join me for tea.'

'Um sure,' I agreed. I was eager to check-in, but it was too early

and my room wouldn't be ready for hours.

'My name is Peter.'

'It's nice to meet you,' I responded. 'My name is Elizabeth Bennett, but my friends call me Lizzie.'

'I see,' Peter nodded while summoning the waiter and putting in an order without asking me what I wanted. 'You didn't return to America for Christmas? Don't you have a family?'

'It's a crazy long story. All the flights home were booked,' I lied. 'As for family, I have so many relatives it's hard to keep them straight. I have four sisters whose names are Jane, Mary, Kitty, and Lydia.'

'I see,' Peter responded stoically. 'You have a large family.'

'My family is Catholic,' I babbled nervously. 'What about you? Are you religious?' I knew the answer was no.

A waiter appeared and gently poured me a cup of chai and set a plate of khanfaroosh — Emirate fried saffron and cardamom cakes — on the table.

'We do not have religion in China. So, Ms. Bennett, what about Mr. Darcy, where is he?'

I almost choked on my tea and asked, 'So you're familiar with Pride and Prejudice?'

Peter was stoic. 'China is a developing country, but we are literate. It's okay if you don't want to tell me your real name, but I do not believe that you have four sisters.'

'Really,' I asked incredulously, 'why is that?'

Peter studied me for a few moments and then remarked, 'You seem like an only child.'

'How can you tell when we've only just met?'

Peter smiled, looked at his watch and said, 'I must go Ms. Bennett, but please join me for a party tomorrow.'

I remained silent. I was too embarrassed to admit that I would be alone for Christmas. I didn't want to appear needy.

Peter got up, paid the bill, and said, 'a car will pick you up tomorrow at 7 p.m.' Then he left.

I suppose it was absurd to get into a stranger's car in a foreign country, but I was overwhelmed by curiosity. I forgot Bonnie's consistent reminders that I was on my own. Should I get into trouble? It was up to me to resolve the situation. Otherwise, I wouldn't be working at Ares VC in Tripoli.

The next day, I wore a dark green dress with a draping neckline, appropriate for any occasion. It was elegant, yet casual. As Peter promised, the hotel front desk messaged me to announce that a driver was waiting to take me to a party.

I was delivered to a skyscraper that looked like a palace. The chauffeur escorted me to the elevator and pressed the button for the penthouse floor. I ascended to an expansive room that looked like a scene from a Pitbull music video.

It was only 7:30 p.m., but the DJ was active while people laughed and danced. The place was smoky and dimly lit so it was hard for me to locate Peter.

I walked through the penthouse towards the infinity pool.

A man approached and said, 'Ahlan wa sahlan.'

'Thank you,' I responded. 'Do you think we could get the DJ to play Hossan Habib's —'

'Soft B'einaya?' the man finished.

'You know that song?' I asked.

'Yes, everyone in the Arab world knows this song.'

I started to ask, 'Isn't Hossan Egyptian?' when I accidentally took a step backward and fell into the swimming pool.

I was shocked. I looked up, and the entire room was staring at me. However, within seconds people were laughing, and returned to whatever they were doing.

Peter emerged from the shadows. Seeing me drenched like a water rat he pulled me out. I was shivering, so he wrapped his blazer around me and escorted me to a back room.

'I'm so embarrassed,' I confessed.

'Don't worry. Kadir likes women who are … What is the word in English?'

'What are you talking about?' I demanded.

'You were flirting with him, yes?'

'Not exactly,' I protested.

'Why don't you shower in my friend's guest room? There should

be a spare robe. I'll have the maids dry your dress.'

'Are you sure they won't mind?'

'Yes, yes, don't worry,' Peter reassured me while escorting me to a guest bathroom at the far end of the penthouse. 'I'll have the servants assist you. You can meet us on the balcony when you feel better.'

'Us?' I asked in confusion.

'Me and my friend who owns this place.'

It was an hour later when I finished drying off. The maids helped me with my dress. I ventured towards the deck and overheard a hushed voice. Peter was speaking Mandarin on his cell.

I heard him say, 'The arms deal is almost complete. We have supplied the necessary capital from Beijing to Moscow. Soon, Gaddafi will have the nuclear missile he needs from Russia.'

I couldn't believe what I was hearing. For months, I had toiled in solitude at Ares without any significant assignments. I felt useless, but suddenly I was privy to information that could determine the future of the entire Arab world, the United States, and most importantly … my career.

I pulled out my phone and did my best to record the last bits of the conversation, but my cell was dead because of the water from the pool.

As soon as Peter got off the phone, I thanked him for his kindness but explained that I felt sick and needed to return to my hotel. I expected him to persuade me to stay, but he nodded sympathetically, walked me downstairs and called the chauffeur.

Opening the door, Peter said firmly, 'I'll see you again.' I nodded. However, I didn't see him again, at least not while I was in Dubai and not when I got back to Tripoli.

I was anxious to report my findings, but no one was at the office in Tripoli and I didn't want to communicate through email. Nevertheless, I messaged Bonnie. She eventually responded, but explained I'd have to wait until the 29th before I could speak to anyone. Apparently, a new VP was arriving and would take over the Tripoli office.

I created a report of what had transpired Christmas Eve. In full detail, I wrote down a description of Peter. I recounted the conversation regarding the Russian arms sale funded by the Chinese, and I listed everything else that could be relevant.

When I saw Bonnie on the morning of the 29th, she was in a good mood. I figured she was excited about the new VP. I was apprehensive about a new boss but hoped he would offer guidance, mentorship, and direction, because I felt lost.

Bonnie listened intently while I described what I witnessed. She was a calm woman and a good listener. Bonnie had been with the company since its inception. In fact, she was one of the first women sent overseas and had worked in Vietnam as a secretary.

I once asked, "What was it like in the early days?"

Bonnie responded, "It was a lot like the television series Mad Men."

After giving Bonnie a detailed account of my adventure, she left to talk with the new VP. I sat alone in her office for ten minutes, but it felt much longer. When she finally returned, I was escorted upstairs to the VP's plush office. The top floor was a stark contrast to my drab spot in the basement.

I was excited to finally prove my value. Surely, now I would have better tasks than reviewing documents in the basement.

As Bonnie opened the VP's office, I saw a man sitting in a chair with his back to the door. He stared out the window. When Bonnie knocked on the door, he spun around and chuckled upon seeing me.

I gasped.

'Thank you, Bonnie, I'll take it from here.' He nodded to her, and she left. 'So, Ms. Bennett we meet again.'

My cheeks reddened upon realizing I was face-to-face with my new neighbor. I stood speechlessly for a minute because I didn't know what to say.

Finally, I stammered, 'You're not Chinese nor from Beijing, are you?' I noticed immediately that Peter had lost all traces of the Chinese accent he had so effortlessly affected a few days ago.

'Nope,' Peter laughed. 'I grew up in Philly. So, Bonnie informed me that you have vital information concerning matters of national security?'

'This was a big joke wasn't it?' I whispered.

'Not at all, Natalia, not at all,' Peter grinned. 'Jokes and hazing? Now that's what I experienced when I served in the military.'

'Prisoners say solitary confinement is worse than physical torture,' I responded indignantly.

He shrugged and said, 'I guess you'd know.'

'No one has called me Natalia in years.'

'I read your file; it explains why we hired you.'

'Why was I selected?' I asked. 'I didn't attend Ivy League Schools or graduate top of my class. Plus, I'm blind without my glasses.'

'God only knows; it was probably an HR error from a system glitch during updates.'

I nodded.

Unexpectedly, a recruiter called me while I was finishing law school. She was most intrigued by the international schools I had attended in Berlin, Istanbul, and Kuala Lumpur. I accepted this job hoping it would help me uncover the truth about my parents. Unfortunately, I didn't learn much except that Mom and Dad had been undercover DEA agents.

Interrupting my thoughts Peter said, 'Cheer up, Lana, your recent sleuthing efforts won't go unrewarded.'

'Really!' I exclaimed, suddenly perking up with hope.

'Yep, come with me,' he ordered. I followed Peter down three flights of stairs to a new office.

As we walked down the hallway, my boss said paternalistically, 'Lana, please be careful … you're very vulnerable.'

'Why do you say that?'

'You have no parents, no siblings, and no close friends. Something could easily happen to you.'

Nervously I attempted to joke, 'I hope that's not a threat.'

'It's a warning,' Peter stated coldly. And, with that, he opened the door to a different room filled with twice the number of boxes that had filled my original office. There were vast mountains of documents.

'Have fun,' he sadistically chuckled as he left me alone and returned to his executive suite upstairs.

As I stood alone in my dreary new cell staring at the endless paperwork, I thought — I'm kind of like the cabin boy in that legal case Queen v. Dudley, Stephens. The 17-year-old victim, Richard Parker was also an orphan and very expendable."

Kevin nodded as he listened to my tale. He stopped scribbling, glanced up and asked, "What was your relationship with Peter Lim?"

"Professional, he was my boss," I stated unequivocally.

"Are you sure about that?" Kevin responded doubtfully.

Tension filled my voice as I declared, "You've heard otherwise?"

Kevin nodded. "There were rumors that the two of you were romantically involved."

"People gossip. I suppose it looked that way because he and I were frequently seen together, especially in the evening at various parties and events."

Kevin nodded.

"It made sense for us to work as a team. Together, we didn't arouse suspicion the way other associates did. We could slip into groups that couldn't be penetrated by others."

"Groups such as …?" Kevin pressed.

"Business groups loyal to Gaddafi."

"Where did the two of you fit in?"

"I have no idea what Peter's genuine political beliefs were," I responded.

"Sure, but the two of you were close."

"Peter Lim's job was to lie. When we worked together in Tripoli, he was loyal to someone who is now the President of a major multi-national corporation. This executive reputedly advised the Gaddafi regime on how to win the "propaganda war." He recommended passing information on potential connections between the rebels and Al Qaeda to the U.S. government. This could be done via American companies in countries such as Israel, Egypt, Jordan, and Morocco."

Kevin said nothing, so I continued talking.

"I had been working on a new project, in the basement, for weeks without seeing much of Peter except in passing. One afternoon, I was

analyzing documents concerning Libyan deals with major oil companies in nations such as Britain, France, and Qatar. Peter called me into his office and said, 'Watch this video.'

Gaddafi was on German television stressing that if Libya was attacked, all energy contracts would be transferred to Russian, Indian, and Chinese companies.

China was Asia's largest purchaser of oil; therefore, it had a significant stake in Libya. It also had more than 75 companies with 36,000 employees in the country, before the civil war. Most were swiftly evacuated in less than three days."

Kevin interrupted me to say, "It must have been difficult for you when Peter left."

"Why do you say that?" I asked.

"Lim did a lot for your career. You were loyal to him."

"I moved from the windowless basement to a bleak office on the first floor," I replied dryly.

"Did you stay in contact with him?"

"No," I replied firmly.

"Have you been in touch with Peter since you moved to China?"

I shook my head and said, "I haven't. Anyway, if I did, wouldn't you know?"

Kevin glared at me but didn't answer my question.

Deferentially I promised, "Peter and I haven't had any email correspondence."

"You have other ways of communicating with him, don't you?" Kevin suggested.

"Why do you say that?" I feigned innocence.

He continued, "Your cryptic posts on social media."

I shrugged and asked, "My literary references?"

Kevin raised an eyebrow.

"Is that a crime? After all, Angleton loved poetry."

"After you've worked here, it's not like you leave to start a bakery," Kevin informed me.

I nodded and said, "Peter was highly educated and well-connected, I'm sure he found a way to survive."

"Yep, he certainly did. I'm sure you know that after the change in administration, Peter and his friends were ousted and left to start their own company."

I was quiet but was keenly aware of the complexities of internal politics.

"Peter's company sells military technology," Kevin responded.

I nodded.

"They've been trading with enemies of the United States such as Russia, Iran, and North Korea for some time. They launder money through Asian real estate companies and international schools."

"What does this have to do with me?"

"We think you're involved," Kevin snapped.

"I'm flattered you think that, but I'm not. Why do you think so?"

"A variety of reasons, but your politics is one reason."

"I have no idea what you mean," I said innocently.

"Don't play games, Lana. We know you openly support arming rogue nations."

I shook my head and clarified, "Not exactly. However, if we support the 2nd Amendment for U.S. citizens, then it's only fair to respect the right of sovereign nations to arm in any manner of their choosing. All men have the right to die with dignity."

"Even Libya?" Kevin asked.

"Yes, especially Libya," I declared with passion. "Gaddafi would still be alive if he had gone nuclear. Benghazi would never have happened. Ambassador Stevens wouldn't have been killed, and what was a flourishing African nation would not be overrun by ISIS."

Kevin raised his hand, indicating that he didn't care to listen to my speech.

"Bank records indicate that you received a substantial sum of money this morning. Care to explain that?"

I didn't say anything because I was startled by his revelation.

"Lana, we believe you're working with Lim and his associates. Did Peter wire you *this* money?"

I paused for a moment, thought rapidly, and then carefully responded, "My cousin Milton died recently. I was his only living relative, and he left me a generous inheritance."

Kevin studied my face for a few minutes. It was as if by looking at me long enough, I might reveal what he wished to know. He appeared vexed that he couldn't detect anything.

I dug my nails into my hidden hands to prevent myself from compressing my lips because that alone would give my interrogator more information than he deserved. I glanced at my watch in an attempt to remind Kevin that I had to get to Curt's office party at the *Bund*.

Kevin was silent for a moment but finally said, "Okay, Lana, you're free to leave. I need to check and verify that your cousin Milton actually died and left you that significant sum of money. Don't go anywhere until I've confirmed your story."

I stood up, smiled and said, "Where on earth would I go?"

END

CHARACTER ANALYSIS

Lana Hayaak/Natalia Canaan

Throughout the story, no one is quite certain about Natalia, except Troy Walker, a Special Forces veteran. Troy says that "abandoned children are damaged." Has she become a corrupt, calculating officer like her father as suggested by both Troy and Aaron?

What does Aaron mean when he leans forward and whispers, "Lana, tell me the truth; you're a drone, aren't you?" Is he referring to the fact that she's the epitome of the bonbon eating lady of leisure or does he know about her role with Ares Venture Capital.

In **Part 1**, Natalia is a fifteen-year-old who has lived a sheltered life overseas. When her parents disappear, she is forced to survive alone in her home country for the first time. She adapts quickly by reacting to situations the way her parents or other expats in her former community would have responded.

In **Part 2**, Natalia is twenty-six but still haunted by her parents' disappearance.

By **Parts 3 & 4**, Natalia is in her early thirties and

behaves with less authenticity than she did in earlier chapters causing readers to wonder if she's become the type of person she once resented.

However, in **Part 5**, other characters, Daniel Petersen, Ben Chang, Priya Patel, and Harold Frost reveal a side of Natalia that she was more political and controversial.

The **Epilogue** exposes Natalia's activities in her late twenties which explains her behavior in **Parts 3 and 4**.

Curt Steiger

Curt is a very ambitious scientist/IP attorney whose primary passion is his work. He appears to be driven only by success and a challenge. At times, Curt is infatuated with Lana, but at other times, she's a complication.

Born in Stuttgart, Germany in the late 70s, Curt immigrated to the U.S. before the fall of the Berlin Wall. His parents were likely born during or in the aftermath of WW2.

Early in the book, when Curt describes Lana, he also mentions his mother: "Lana reminded me of one of the actresses in the black and white films my mother watched on TCM."

In **Part 3**, Lana mentions that his mother died in 2012. In the end, we learn that Curt's mother escaped from East Berlin when she was a teenager.

Ben Chang

Ben Chang is a focused business partner whose primary concern is the maximization of corporate profits. With Lana, he is kind, gentle, and supportive. However, in the end, he is most pleased by her departure because she was created conflict.

Ben and Cindy's grandparents were wealthy opium dealers who fled China during the revolution.

Cindy Han

We're first introduced to Cindy in **Part 2** when she goes to a popular club in the Bund to learn more about Lana. Later, she quarrels with someone on the phone about Lana and the reader is left to wonder if the speaker was Curt or Ben.

Cindy first meets Lana to 'rescue' her. Initially, Lana drops her guard for women like Cindy and Amy in. However, by the end of **Part 2**, Lana's admiration is replaced with distrust.

Some describe Cindy as a strong businesswoman whose interest in Curt was driven mainly by her stake in their pharmaceutical company.

Aaron Walker

Aaron Walker is an uncomplicated man from the Midwest who enjoys simple pleasures such as hunting and fishing. He possesses more insight into human nature than any of the other characters.

Amy Liu

Amy is from a well-connected Beijing family, who did not leave during the revolution.

As Cindy's best friend, Amy is the voice of reason. With Lana, she is kind. In the end, is Amy's wedding toast intended to be a joke?

Peter Lim

Through Lana's eyes, we learn about the Vice President of Ares Venture Capital — Peter Lim. Lana describes Peter's first test, but we can presume there were subsequent tests.

Physically, he resembles Jason Canaan. Like, Lana's father, he grew up on the East coast, served in the military, is well-educated, and played both sides of the political game.

Daniel Petersen

When Lana first meets Daniel in the Korean airport, he is a baby-faced young man full of enthusiasm. By the end of Part 4, he has put on fifty pounds and grown a beard but is still bursting with optimism. He tells Lana that she needs someone who will make her laugh and for once she agrees with him.

As Lana is running off the train, she says "Sorry, Daniel … I'm no Batman; I'm no hero." Throughout the book, the only heroic type of character is Daniel who attempts to save the "damsel in distress." But arguably, he is an interventionist who fails to solve any problems and is driven by a false narrative.

ENDING ANALYSIS

Lana's future in Libya is hinted at in the beginning of **Part 2** when Curt describes her conversation with a law professor. According to Curt, she questions Professor Fitzgerald's syllabus, but then asks: "What was it like to represent ..." The North African leader's name isn't mentioned, but we can presume it was Gaddafi.

Lana is lying about the money wired to her account because at the end of **Part 1** she describes her cousin Milton's money problems and four children to two different wives.

ABOUT LICIA FLYNN

Licia Flynn grew up attending international schools and obtained a Juris Doctor from a law school in Silicon Valley. Her undergrad focus was political theory and military history.

On her maternal side, Licia is descended from Irish immigrants who arrived at the Port of New Orleans in the 1800s and survived by teaching math, fighting wars, and telling tales.

Licia's paternal grandparents were educated merchants who fled China in the 1940s.

www.instagram.com/liciaflynn
www.facebook.com/FirmResolveLiciaFlynn
www.twitter.com/FirmResolve
www.klar-marketing.com

FIRM DENIAL
Now Available

During a trip to Hong Kong, Daniel Petersen hunts down Aaron Walker. The men develop an offbeat friendship as the Iraq vet describes events in Shanghai that contradict Lana's account in Firm Resolve.

Meanwhile, near Central Asia, an enigmatic sighting arouses controversy and threatens national security.

Email a copy of your book review to LiciaFlynn@gmail.com and receive a FREE copy of Firm Denial (United States Only).

FIRM
DENIAL
Licia Flynn

Available
2019